THE BREAKUP

Brooke Gantt

THE BREAKUP

For information, contact www.ModelShrink.com

WBM Publishing

ISBN-13: 978-1542398794

Table of Contents

DEDICATION

To all women who want to break up with their significant other but don't know why they stay – You are not alone.

Prologue

I squint at the setting sun and mumble under my breath as I search in my handbag for my keys. I'm standing in front of my parent's building, but as always, I find something to delay me and hold off going inside. I like to think I'm wary of my mother but deep down, I know what I really feel towards her and that is sheer, undiluted terror. Dad and I are pals and he, coupled with my beautiful niece, whom I love dearly, are the only reasons I still come here.

I focus on my handbag; there's a lot of junk inside it and even though I keep saying I'll clear it all out, I never end up doing so. I hiss impatiently, as my search turns up a scrunched up receipt for a cute, multi-colored pair of socks I saw in the department store window close to my apartment last month, and couldn't resist buying. I throw it back into the bag and dip my fingers inside again; out comes an old gum wrapper, a felt-tip pen that I haven't used in ages, my grocery shopping list, a tiny jotter I take everywhere I go, because you never know when a great idea will pop into your head like Jerry from Tom & Jerry - the jotter ensures I always catch the idea by its tail, before it darts out again -, an old earring, and finally! Ah, I can touch the keys. I drag my hand out triumphantly only to see it's not my keys, but the keys to my boyfriend's 2004 dirty Chevy.

"Urgh!" I exclaim, my breath wheezing out in disgust, as I slam the car keys on the hood of my boyfriend's car. I'm about to go all the way and take my frustration out on the poor car by slamming my foot against its tires, but luckily common sense prevails and stops me just in time. The keys will turn up somewhere soon, but in the meantime, I get into the car and decide to not go into my parent's house after all and drive over to my boyfriend's house instead because I'm certain I gave him my spare keys, even though he has never used it I'm sure it's in his bowl of things he needs that sits on his shelf. The excuse to avoid seeing my mother rings hollow even to my ears. I stubbornly shrug it off as I hear sounds of police sirens speeding passed me. It was quite weird. The neighbourhood is as peaceful as still waters, except for my parent's frequent squabbles. I wondered who the police had come for, and after I couldn't guess, I resigned to saying a silent prayer for them.

Not long afterward, I noticed three uniform men of different ranks standing not far from my parent's place. I step out of my car and my purse drops from my shoulder lying in the cup of my forearm. A cold chill ran through my spine at the thought of what might be happening. I calmed down and cautiously approached the sidewalk. "You will stand back miss," a stern voice shouted at me, as officers ran into my parents building. The officer with the stern voice had his hand on his gun holster as if I was a criminal. The nosey next door neighbours were all up in my business now, but I was too busy to pay them any mind, as I had my eyes fixed on the cop. I swing all twenty-two inches of my wavy nut brown hair to my backside allowing room to place my purse back on my shoulder.

"My parents and niece live in there," I pointed out to the average built officer. The officer questioned me asking what my parent's names are, which apartment do they live in…? I glared at his jaded jade eyes. He was ready to take down anyone including victims, as my sister darted out of the building accompanied by my mother, my niece wrapped tightly in my mother's arms bawling uncontrollably.

I haven't seen my sister for a few years now. Her last episode at the mental hospital made it clear she was not coming out anytime soon, but it was obvious she was here to get her daughter back. Long overdue is an understatement. I hate the fact she had to leave my niece with my mom. On the day my niece and her half-brother were to be released to my mom, my sister's 8-year-old stepson pulled the social worker to the side and said he rather be with strangers than to be with my mom. He was sent to another family. My niece was too young to make a decision. My dad and I are here to protect her until she is old enough to be on her own.

"Cuff her!" I heard one of the men say who I decided was the detective say to the officer with jaded eyes. Instead, the officer released and grabs his handgun pointing it at my sister. "Stand down officer!" the detective said. The officer ignored the command. "Stand down!" the detective repeated. Usually, I play the role of referee and arbitrator in my family arguments, but as I stood watching that late afternoon, I was certain the situation was more than just an argument, and the officer with the jaded eyes was out to kill. "I'm going to ask you one more time to stand down, officer!" He finally placed his gun back in his holster and like a virus, the news had spread throughout the entire neighbourhood, turning our place into a tourist attraction.

"Miss, I'm Detective Shawl. What is your name? Do you live in this building?" he said. Bombarded with more questions? I have some of my own. "Where is my dad? Do you believe in police brutality? Your officer was about to take down my sister!" The detective looked at me with disgust and said, "He was just doing his job." Right then and there I knew the law was not on my side.

"Everyone is fine," the detective continued. "Cliff and is wife-" I was sure he said my sister's husband is here as I interrupted with a trembling voice, "What?! My sister's husband is here!" The detective looked towards my niece and said, "From what I have learned so far, they came to take their daughter back which turned into a heated altercation. The police were called just in time. Everything is under control." I could tell he was not telling me everything, my sister screaming, "I want my lawyer!" They shoved my helpless handcuffed sister along the newly cut grass, my niece kicking and crying simultaneously now in an officer's arms with jet black hair.

"Glory!" I shouted to my niece. The officer with the jet black hair strutted towards me. "Stay away from my grandbaby!" my mom said to me. The bewildered officer stepped back as I reminded my mom that Glory is my niece. My dad angrily reminding her as well and he shouted to my mom from the front of the building. I was so happy to see my dad was okay. "Stop acting like a crazy woman." He grabbed my niece from the officer with ebony hair and marched in my direction. "Shut up goofball," my mom said. "Something is seriously wrong with you woman, can someone put her in the police car?" my dad said. My mom roller's sprung from her head as she charged towards me while yelling at my dad a few steps away from her, "Oh yeah take her side like you always do, you low life piece of crap." She turns and looks me straight in my eyes and says, "I hate you." I moved back concerned for my niece.

My mom certainly thought this is my fault, as was every other family mishap. "Why do you treat me this way?! You should be talking to my sister and her husband like this. They are the crazy ones who caused Glory to be taken away," I reminded. "Liar! I don't trust you, not one bit!" my mom said lunging and grabbing my arm, shaking me as she slapped me in my face releasing me from her grip. Naturally, I held my sore cheek and it took no time before I fell to the ground and hit my head on the concrete ground. I was knocked out cold right there. "Mam!" the puzzled detective shouted, the officers holding my mom off me. Eventually regaining consciousness, I swung my head here and there to regain focus. Blurred figures stand around me were all I managed to see and the voices that came from the mouths of the blurred figures sounded distorted.

"Help me!" I cried, as splattered crimson blood rushed from my arm while I lay there drifting into unconsciousness.

* * * * *

Several beautiful encouraging and hopeful words filled the air, and some of them even coming from unexpected people like my mom as I lay there in silence, with my eyes still closed. The words that soothed me the most were the words from my dad's mouth. They were most sincere. From the conversation I overheard, I knew I was at the hospital.

The doctor had sometimes come for updates. The last update was that I miraculously made it through my operation and was okay to go home. He then mentioned something like "bullet," but I failed to understand it, so I listened on. According to him, I had been shot, and the bullet had hit an artery in my arm, therefore; I won't be able to use my arm for a month. Otherwise, I risk losing my thumb if the artery didn't heal correctly. My dad suggested I stay at the house with them, as the doctor handed my dad a manila envelope. "This is for your daughter. It's the results of her pregnancy test," the doctor said, my mother ripping the envelope from my dad's hands. "Let me see this!" she exclaimed. *Pregnancy test?* I thought to myself. I slowly opened my eyes with hazy vision, lifting my injured arm engulfed in a cast. "Ouch!" I shouted in agonizing pain. My parents rushed to my aid. My niece and my boyfriend nowhere to be found.

* * * * *

The drive home was filled with nothing but unanswered questions. *My mom only slapped me how did I end up on the ground with a bullet in my arm? Who would want to shoot me? Where is the pregnancy test? Did my mom see the results? Well, I doubt it. Although I'm grown she still thinks I'm a child so if she has the results and it was positive she would have cut up my head in 50,000 pieces by now simply because I'm not married,* I thought to myself.

7

My mom thanks God for my recovery and then calls my dad all sort of names. I still couldn't understand how there was a shooting in broad daylight right under the noses of the cops. What I also could not believe was that I just moved into my own place after a few years of living home with my parents, and now I was stuck in the house again with my mom for the next month or so.

The car finally became quiet, and I dosed off to sleep still exhausted from the drugs the doctor administered. Thirty minutes later we arrived at my parents' place, but before parking the car, my father yelled, "Oh man!" "What!" my mom screamed. "A black cat just ran in front of my car. I got enough bad luck in my life. I don't need anymore," my dad continued. "If you had Jesus in your life you wouldn't worry about bad luck," my mom informed. Great now he got her started again, as he reverses his car to break the cat's line at least this is what he was told to do when this sort of thing happens. I don't believe in bad luck either but I do remember the Black Out in New York City. On my way to a casting, I had just walked under a latter and all the lights in Manhattan went out, so I got to wonder, and I rubbed my bed ridden eyes and yelled to my dad, "Back up the car again dad," I chuckled.

Meanwhile, my mother chatters on the phone to family and then to the detective. He claimed they were done with the investigation since they found a pistol in Cliff's hand. They believed he shot me and according to Cliff right before he was shot down by the police he claimed, the bullet was meant for my mother who took their daughter. That was the motive and that was the story they were sticking with.

Entering my parent's home, I stared around. The place will never be the same again. My sister's husband was apparently responsible for this as I looked at where he was shot and every other place or object loved. They had cleaned up as much as possible, but the atmosphere and air stank of what happened. I thought what a messed up, and abusive husband my sister had, but I never thought he was capable of murder.

My mind drifted to when my boyfriend Jay-O and I met and I smiled dreamily, as I saw the unopened envelope with the pregnancy results hanging out of my mom's handbag. I grabbed it and ripped it open, reading the results. I heard a knock at the door and it was him, my boyfriend. He kissed me and I kissed him back, nervously throwing the envelope on the table. He had a concerned look on his face. I did not want to worry my boyfriend, so I told him my injury was just a flesh wound. "Yeah, yeah, cool," he said as if he didn't care. I followed his eyes to see what he did care about. He was staring at the envelope and the words pregnancy test as big as day stared back at him.

"Are you pregnant?" he asked. "Shh my parents are in the other room," I informed. "I asked you a question," he said. I ignored him and wrapped my arms around him so tight, laying my head on his shoulder, closing my eyes and smiled. He grew more elusive than what I bargained for, pushing me away and yelled, "Answer me!" I grabbed my injured arm. He calmed down, held me and said, "I'm sorry." I forgave him like I always do. I was just so happy to see him but there was one problem as I looked up from my boyfriend's embrace and asked, "What is she doing here?"

Chapter 1
FIVE YEARS EARLIER

My life had taken a dangerous turn. A very dangerous turn. Despair was only one of the things I wallowed in. It had crept in like a mouse at night and had gradually begun to eat deep into the fibre of my very existence. It gripped me so firmly as it spread over me that I knew it had come to stay. Then it systematically invited its other friends in one at a time. Sadness was the first of them. It joined despair in tearing down my system and then came distaste, withdrawal and then some.

My self-esteem had been badly dented for sure. If I had not already lost the last shred of my confidence, I was definitely holding on to that last shred. The things my mirror told me about myself weren't so good, or was it the things I chose to see? I can't say for sure. I had always been a stand-up girl and confident person, but it was impossible to hold on to all that self-assurance after more than six men had fallen out of love with me in the space of two years. Though a part of me was almost sure they were all punks and didn't deserve a good woman like me. Yes, I'm a good woman. I'd readily do anything to please my man, that's, of course, asides getting pregnant for him - not at this point in my career, I can't handle the weight gain now, nah.

I continued to struggle with my self-esteem, and I was becoming more withdrawn by the day. Each day I would spend several minutes in front of the standing mirror at the north end of my room, checking myself out and assessing my features just to decide if I was probably getting old and losing my charm. You couldn't blame me much, though. Kelvin – my wannabe rock star who had just left me had left in a very dramatic manner. His last words insinuated the possibility that I was no longer as desirable, but then, is that what love is about? Looking desirable? I thought we were together for good and bad. Anyway, Kelvin's words left a sharp sting, one that had me second guessing myself each time the memory came back with his wickedly sexy husky voice ringing at the back of my head, "You blame me for cheating with that girl? Apart from you not having enough time for us, she's got the greatest body I've ever seen." I think that was too cruel of him to say; I believe it was just to spite me. On the other hand, he admitted he detest women and his reasoning is based on his high school sweetheart cheating on him. The bottom line is Kelvin is damaged goods and he wanted too much of my time and I couldn't give that to him. I mean, I tried, but he was too lazy and idle, and there was no way I could deal with that.

I hated myself too, yeah, that was that? I hated myself for many things. The fact that I still hadn't learnt from the many mistakes before him, so;

therefore; I despised myself for allowing myself to roll with such a brute as Kelvin. There was no doubt that I picked the worst choices in men.

After things had ended with Kelvin, I took a break from my career as a model and actress and left New York City to move in with my parents, and for three years, I remained single and wrote. I was going through a phase I'll like to call regrouping. I had ample time to reflect on my choices and decisions. Also, during this time I considered taking a 9 to 5 job using my Master's in business, but then an opportunity relaunched itself in the form of a play I had written a year ago called *Men*. I want to use this as a platform to help others get over a bad relationship. I am to produce this play alongside my good friend Jason. Jason wanted me to perform the play, but I was still on a sabbatical so I wanted to be behind the scene instead. Besides, it was time to give way to the younger generation. They too deserved a chance to shine, and it will be fulfilling if I could be a part of someone's success story.

"Thank you Amber, you did great! See you tomorrow," I said. "Same time, same place?" Amber assumed. "Actually, we are meeting downtown at my grandma's building tomorrow at 1 o'clock. She has a meeting room so I can record you for a nationwide talent show, remember we had this discussion?" I said, as I reapplied my lip gloss. "Oh, it's tomorrow? Okay I will be there. I don't have to work," Amber said prancing out the front door. "This is when I wish I were back in New York working with serious actresses," I mumbled. "What was that Sookie," Jason laughed, galloping down his staircase. Sookie was his nickname for me. "Anyways, I know he heard me," I murmured. "So how did your rehearsal go," Jason wondered. "It went well, but I'm glad we are having the show at your house instead of at a huge theatre because I don't think Amber is ready for a big crowd," I admitted.

"You know Sookie if you ask me-" "Here we go," I interrupted. "I'll say you're the best person to act in the play, if for no other reason, for the singular fact that you wrote the story and no-one else could interpret it like you will, what more, you're full of grace and elegance; it will be such a delight to watch," he continued. Jason was sitting on his gray soft leather two seater somewhere on the east side of his place, looking out the window, and letting beams of daylight creep in through the lowered frames. If he hadn't mentioned my name, I would think he was talking to the air. Jason did that a lot. He liked to look elsewhere when persuading you to do something you'll ordinarily not do. "You need to stop trying to change my mind; I won't bulge. Life is real and one of the reasons I don't want to do it is because I'm too old for these things now." He smiled wryly, as though he had just listened to an empty threat ever. I hated the look of his smile, but I didn't let it get to me, especially since my mind was made up.

"Old you say? How could you say old? Is that even a word that should be used in association with you, when you're looking 21 and sexy?" he said, "but seriously, how old are you now? I have known you ever since you were 16-years-old. You got to be in your fifties now." I grunted, plopping next to him, getting cosy. He definitely keeps himself looking and smelling good, and just like that, his eyes met mine as if he wanted to kiss me like we use to do back in the day, shoving him away and I said, "You see that. You know my age is classified information, but if I'm in my fifties you must be in your sixties, But you can't tell because you got that bald head so no one can see that your hair matches this couch." Jason knew I stopped him right in his tracks. He is just as secretive about his age as I am. You got to be in the entertainment business.

"Don't forget tall dark and chocolate, and these muscles the ladies die for," Jason said, flexing his arm, cheesing with his bright pearly teeth. He was trying to be funny now, and I played along. "By the way, I don't look 21 Jason, I look 19, and I always will be 19 forever," I replied, and we both laughed. I laughed, not because the joke was that funny, but because I was happy to have a cool person around me again. I was also glad to have something that kept me busy now, and that was helping me to mend my downcast mood. I seemed to be back on the right path, and on the brink of what was to be a big break if things went to plan. A break that could shoot me back high in my almost dead career, even though I had my fears, and doubts still.

On another note, I updated Jason on my love life. I explained to him when I moved back in with my parents three years ago two of those years I spotted a guy I like who works at the electronic store across the street from my grandma's building, but after Kelvin and I split I was struggling with an abysmally low self-esteem at that time, as I had yet to shake off Kelvin's words and the wrong notion they gave me about myself. So, even though the guy from across the street from my grandma's eventually gathered the courage to ask for my digits after staring at me for two years, I was almost sure there was no hope of us getting anywhere. Not to mention, we were from totally different worlds. Me being a mixed black girl, and him a Japanese guy. Secondly, I'm older, living with my parents, with no job. A few things that made Jason think it wasn't a good idea at all. To him, it was just going to be another bad relationship, but now he knows why I have rehearsal at my grandma's building tomorrow. I'm headed to see the guy across the street afterwards.

Anyhow, I didn't agree with Jason's assessment. I don't think my situation, my age or racial difference means anything if two people really want to be together, but who was I kidding. The guy and I hardly talked or knew anything about each other. All we ever did was stare from awkward angles every time our paths crossed, and not to mention I did not have a chance to give him my number when he asked. He probably thinks I'm stuck up or playing hard to get. One thing was for sure; I like him. He seems like the kind of man I need in my life. A nice regular guy. Not a rock star, a wannabe rock star, or a millionaire. A man who has his life together or at least a simple life, working and not lying down. And now things have changed for me. I will go for him and see if we can get anywhere, and that's that, as I remembered what my dad said to me, 'Go out, see new places, meet new people with positive vibes, and refresh your mind,' those were my dad's exact words. My dad always looked out for me. I will conveniently choose him over my mother any day of the week. He hardly feels bad when I tell him about my relationship woes. He always has something cheerful to say, always encouraging me to look on the bright side. Now that I think about it, I believe he found it easy to deal with my heartbreaks because he's a man. He probably knows how messed up his kind are, and how it is never really a woman's fault that she can't make him stay.

Moving on, my grandmother is very nosy. She had caught me looking at the guy from across the street one day, and she never stopped talking about it since. She kept asking why we were both stalling, and eventually, she told me, "A week ago I left your man crush a note with your digits since you both are too cowardly to make a move."

Now I had more of a reason to see this guy. I had let myself wallow in depression long enough, and on a bright Tuesday morning, after my rehearsal and apparently a week after my grandma gave the guy my number and his call hadn't come, I set out to meet him at his store to see what was the hold-up, but unluckily, his co-worker with a strong accent said Jingguo wasn't in. *Jay-O, oh, that is his name*, I thought to myself. "Jay-O is not in?" I repeated. His co-worker smiled as if I said something wrong. Nonetheless, I'll have to wait for another time to meet him, if I ever got the courage. Of course, I never did get the courage to confront him again, just as he never got enough to call me.

It was a warm Friday afternoon, I had received several calls from Jason discussing the details for the play - and a text message saying I had a meeting downtown with a prospective sponsor later in the evening, I turned my closet on its head in search of something professional but sexy to wear, and then I stood in front of the mirror for almost an hour. I could hardly decide what shade of lipstick was perfect to go with my outfit, or what kind of footwear to put on, or if I needed sunglasses or my red Gucci jacket. I felt a heavy burden weighing down on my shoulders and making them sag resultantly. I had never been so confused about what to wear, nor had I ever feared so much to appear awkward before a sponsor. Moments later, I finally picked out an outfit, as I put the finishing touches on my make-up.

I stepped out a few minutes after 4:00 pm and headed to the location. That was quite early, I had till 6:30 pm before the meeting, that's what the text message read. So, I wandered around the city for a bit, ending up at a pub, where I took a seat by the window so I could watch the street from inside and see what went on. Not that there was anything intriguing to watch, but watching as people sauntered here and there, crossing the roads, making phone calls, holding hands and smiling despite the many troubles they hid under their clothes was way more fun than having to look at the tired and indifferent faces of the grumpy old men in the pub.

Eventually, I ordered some food that I could hardly eat. Something about the streets seemed to fascinate me. It seemed as though I saw things I had never seen before in a very detailed way. Then my eyes caught a guy, and I lost my appetite on the spot. My tummy felt full, and it was impossible to stop my eyes from feasting on him. He is such a looker, better still; he's the guy from the electronic store. I traced his every step with my stationed eyes as I prayed that he will come into the pub.

My prayers were answered in earnest, and he headed for the pub. Then I began to wish he would at least notice me like he does at the store and come over to my table so I could perceive his scent. I lost interest in watching the street. It seemed like a pretty boring thing to do with the presence of Jay-O inside. I didn't look up from my table, but I sure spied on him from under my eyelids. A small part of my appetite returned and I resumed to my food. Each trip my hand made from my plate to my mouth was laden with a thousand and one thoughts, each of which had Jay-O written all over it. It was dangerous, I knew, to allow myself to get so carried away about this guy was not a good thing, but there was nothing I could do about it anymore, it had already continued like that for too long. I had been thrown off balance, and before this very moment I had found myself shamelessly fantasizing about him several nights against my better judgement.

"I figured you might never forgive me if I left without making a stop here first." I was startled out of my trance. I was no longer the only one at my table, and the voice I heard was positively masculine. I have not looked from my plate, so I didn't know whose voice it was yet. A small shadow of what seemed like a head danced around on my table, covering a small portion of my plate with a mild darkness. I slowly raised my head and when I was done, I was more than happy to see who it was that had said those words. I stood up and gave him a nervous but welcoming hug. I didn't know if a mild smile would suffice, or laughter. I pinched myself mentally and quickly thought of an appropriate response. "Sorry? I don't quite follow," as we both sat down. He cleared his throat and said, "I saw you staring before I entered this place, just as you always do when you are in my store. I was staring too. I guess this is the perfect opportunity we both needed."

I was smitten. I am quite sure, that none of the things I said that afternoon made much sense. His presence was so imposing and hard to fight. Although he came across as shy when I saw him at the store, he wasn't shy now, so I just let him talk and allowed myself to enjoy it.

I was late for my meeting. The truth is, I almost totally forgot I had a meeting. The excitement was almost too much to contain. I was sitting with the guy from the electronic store, in person, after months of staring and wishing, and from years of feeling used and unwanted by men, and then being alone; Jay-O came through for me when I was on the threshold of losing my sanity. Quite a saviour.

I noticed his cell phone lying on the table so I gathered enough nerve to ask, "Did my grandmother give you a note with my number?" mostly because I didn't know what to say, and he answered, "No, can I have it now?" I was surprised, but I hid it well. I wondered why my grandma would tell such a lie. I proceeded to give him my number and when he punched in the first three numbers on his phone, it read, 'Sexy granddaughter,' at least that's what I could see from reading it upside downtown from across the table. "Oh yeah, I do have your number. I texted you several times but you never responded," he said. I laughed. "That's because it's a landline," I replied. He smiled. "I thought your grandmother gave me the wrong number," as I caught him staring at another woman for a moment, before coming back to me. *He's a womaniser,* I thought to myself. *Nah, he is one of the nice ones. Besides men can look*, as my encounter with the guy ended. I had to rush to my meeting.

After my meeting, I thought about my moment at the pub with Jay-O and although we had an enjoyable time I came to the conclusion that Jason is right about my having been in bad relationships. An idea came to mind, and on impulse, I went to the nearest supermarket to buy a diary. I'm going to write about me and Jay-O's potential love story. It feels silly but I have always wanted a diary anyway, and now seemed a good time. Growing up, the fear that my mother would find my diary and hound me over it had kept me from keeping one.

I arrive at my house, my parents are picking up my niece and won't be back until night, so I pour a glass of wine and curl up in my dad's armchair. I reach for my diary and settle in my seat. This seat used to be dad's favorite, but now I have taken over it and he has moved to the one facing the fireplace. I rubbed lovingly at the back of the navy-blue diary and opened it. There's a tiny blue pen hooked in the inside of it. I removed the pen and flipped to the beginning of the journal. I'm going to write forwards, or is it backward?

I write my first words, a little uncertainly.

My name is Monroe Kennedy and I am an actress, script-writer, and model.

From this point on, I'm going to write monthly reports on my possible relationship with Jay-O, so I can look back and see clearly if things start to go wrong.

Chapter 2 - APRIL

Things started happening after our unplanned date. Jay-O called me later in the evening to make sure my meeting with the sponsor went well. How very sweet of him. We talked about many things, amongst clarifying that his name is "Jingguo" after I called him Jay-O a few times during our conversation. I had always heard his co-workers call him Jay-O in the store, but it made sense, since the name of the electronic store is *E-Jing-Tronics*, and that also meant he owned the store. "I guess your employees' accents are too strong," I teased. "It was only a misconception and I prefer Jay-O to Jingguo anyway," he said, and he permitted me to call him Jay-O. How could he not?

Jay-O and I continued to call and exchange text messages, getting to know more about each other with each call and text. I felt so comfortable talking to him, and I will give him credit for that. He was quite easy to talk too. I explained to him my reasons for moving out of New York and in with my parents, against my wishes. I also bragged one evening about my upcoming play and how I was soon to become a great writer.

I couldn't go a day without hearing Jay-O's voice for at least thirty minutes on the phone. I somehow preferred his voice on the phone then in person. There was a sweet tinge to it on the phone. We spoke about our favorite foods and then his origin. "I like sushi especially the Volcano. I guess you like sushi too since you are Japanese," I assumed. "I'm Chinese, you thought I was Japanese?" he said. "I had heard people call you all sorts of things from Japanese to Philippine to Hawaiian," I replied. He was so hysterical, and it amused me. We chit-chatted more about foods, and I found out he is a vegetarian, but eats fish and loves sushi but hates Chinese food. I almost couldn't understand it, but I let it pass. We eventually set a date, and I was more than excited about how it would be on our first official date. I told myself I might just have to create a list of things to talk about this time, lest I lose my voice like at the pub.

* * * * *

I was sitting in a chair right in front of the window so that I will not miss Jay-O when he eventually arrived if he got the directions I gave him correctly. I was jumpy and angry at the same time. He is two hours late, and I feared my dress might begin to get soaked with sweat soon. He had called to tell me he was held up in traffic, but that wasn't enough to calm my nerves. I logged in to my laptop and googled out of impatience and typed, what to do if a man is running late for a date. I found the many suggestions funny, but one said as long as the guy calls, one should exercise patience, as I saw Jay-O speed pass my place, then backing up in reverse, and facing the wrong way - on a one-way street.

I stepped out in my icy blue spring dress. My hair was brushing against my skin as I made eye contact with my neighbor as if I did not see Jay-O. "Hi, Ms. Jordon," I said, waving. She turned her head peeking at Jay-O and whispered across the street, "He's cute." I strutted towards Jay-O's vehicle and instead of getting out the car, he leaned over from the driver's seat to open my door. Annoyed I sat down but smiled. I could tell he was nervous and must have smoked a pack of cigarettes from the smell of his messy car just as messy as my mom keeps her car. He wore an emerald shirt and a pair of worn blue jeans and shoes. I pointed him in the direction of the restaurant, and off we went.

Once we were seated at the restaurant, I couldn't order my favorite wine since he forgot his license. He insisted I order a glass and refused to take a sip from mine after offering it to him several times. Jay-O slipped back into being the shy guy I saw at the store. He didn't seem ready to talk at all. He was satisfied just looking at me, and unsure of what to say his first utterance was that I tell him more about myself. It sounded like a job interview - so formal. Moreover, we had done plenty of that over the phone already. I knew I had to step it up and save the day, or this date will go down in my diary as a disaster. I finally convinced him to take a sip of my wine to get him tipsy and loosen his tongue. It worked, and he confessed he was awed by my beauty and that he couldn't find words to say. Jay-O did manage to confess to having four girlfriends which he claimed to have dumped before meeting me tonight. I didn't want to discuss that, lest I sounded jealous or possessive.

We had fun all through the night; I made sure of it. He told me more about his Asian decent and his name. We laughed about me changing his name to Jay-O from Jingguo. We also gabbed more about my upcoming play and how I became a model and actress in New York City and then a writer. I explained to him I'm still a model and actress but I focus mainly on writing. I also mentioned my intention to buy a house not too far from his neighborhood. This impressed him, as he lived in a very wealthy area.

Then he proceeded to say, "My parents live in China, but I was raised in DC with my aunt and uncle who are millionaires. My parents thought my brother and I would be better off so I shuttled between them both while growing up. I can hardly even speak any Chinese, and I get ashamed whenever I go home. My younger brother is a doctor living in DC. The electronic store had belonged to my aunt before she willed it over to me here in Philly. My aunt wanted me to get a house after taking ownership of the store, but I preferred a condo, especially since I found one that overlooks the harbor. I'm just 29-years-old, in case you're wondering. By the way, how old are you?" I smiled at the question; I was so sure not to answer him. I told him its classified information, and we laughed. He got quiet again but then a few minutes later his shyness left his body and we had been chatting for thirty minutes straight, and I enjoyed watching him talk so much that I didn't want him to stop.

I understood why he had no accent now; he'd never lived at home. I liked the fact that he had such responsibility as overseeing such a big store at his very young age, and I smiled at how I used to think he was only a cashier. We hardly ate our food. There was too much talking, and we ended up closing down the restaurant and another one across the street from there. We got exhausted eventually and instead of going to another restaurant we headed for his car.

This time, Jay-O opened the door for me. He drove me back home that night, oh, and he was quite a gentleman, although he may have been pretending to be, it felt very cool. What was even cooler was Jay-O not making any attempt to lay hands on me. He didn't as much as lean in for a kiss. We chatted more after that date, and we fixed other dates, which he cancelled, on two occasions, his excuse being that he had issues to sort with his employees. According to him, one of them was in a car accident. I was too impatient and I sent him a text, telling him to make me a priority. That may be perceived as a bit too pushy, but it got the desired results. Jay-O fixed another date quickly, and this time, he didn't cancel. He picked me up and I saw a bright yellow nail file with flowers on it in his car, but I said nothing of it. I was yet to be his girlfriend, and so there were limits.

On this date, we went to the movies. No kissing or holding hands. He did manage to leave the movie to answer a couple of phone calls. Never knew who it was.

I decided although we had a great conversation he was definitely shy but by the third date, it was obvious he wasn't shy, he was sweet like that. Jay-O was taking it quite slow, so slow I cannot picture him having sex. He seemed so innocent looking, and that was impressive. While at dinner, he sat on the same side of the table with me and he continued to tell me more about himself and I told him about me leaving a little mystery. He invited me to Paris for a wedding, in October, oh how romantic. And even though I would like to be with a regular guy and not a millionaire Jay-O is such a sweet, kind, sensitive, down-to-earth person with an old soul, like a care bear, and yes, he is a looker but I won't say he's much of a handsome man, but there was something about the way he carried himself that made him good looking and to die for. I knew I was stuck, and it might take some serious disappointments to get me out of his grasp.

* * * * *

"You moronic old man, when will you ever be useful? How did you manage to burn the food for peat's sake?" That was my mom talking to my dad. I doubt if there's anyone above ground who is as abusive as my mom. She was always on my dad's case. She had asked him, of course not nicely, to help keep an eye on the food she had in the microwave, and it had got slightly burnt eventually. That is because she asked my dad to help her bring some boxes down from her closet at the same time he was supposed to be monitoring the food. There was no single name she didn't call my dad. But he handled it well. Aside from occasionally laying her out he mostly didn't say anything asides "sorry," and I think that made her even more agitated. My mom couldn't deal with people who had the ability to keep calm in the face of her torment. I have always wanted to ask my dad how he had managed to live with her this long without strangling her or something like that, but I never got around to ask.

It was a Saturday morning, and I had come to visit them after so much bickering from my mom about me not spending time with my family. Glory had been clamouring to see me too, and I can say she was the reason I went eventually. If I had a choice, I wouldn't see my mom more than once or twice in a year at most. You have to be psychologically ready for her drama before visiting her. "Mother, cut dad some slack will you; you don't expect him to be in two places at the same time now, do you?" I shot at her, bracing up for her response. You could never go scot free when you attack my mom. "If you don't know what to do with your mouth, you'd better shut it up. This is between my husband and me." I smiled. It was all I could do. My mom is a sweet woman, she has a good heart, but her actions are not anywhere near convincing as she bickered with me non-stop.

Sometime later, I called out to my niece, "Glory, come on let's go out for some air." She was busy peeking through my bag at one corner of the house. I hated for her to witness quarrels and fights between my parents or between my mom and me. She was used to it by now already, but I just couldn't stand it when I'm around. Glory jumped up and joined me where I waited at the doorway; then I sent her back to get my purse from my bag. I wanted to take her somewhere nice, away from all the brutality at home. "Don't grab that Glory! It's too heavy!" My mom called to her, as I stared at my mom in disgust. "Yes, mom," Glory said sadly. "It's okay, my purse is not heavy," I informed. "No! She cannot pick that up. She may hurt herself," my mother said grabbing my purse. "Oh what a lovely bag," she said, with a calmer tone.

Before leaving, though, I wanted to make sure my dad was okay and I knew the only place to find my father apart from the kitchen was his bedroom. So, I wandered towards his room, where I found him resting and listening to music on his tablet with headphones to drain my mom's chaos. His bedsheet was stained with colorful markers - that was clearly Glory's doing. I tapped him slightly and watched him jump up like he had a bad dream, rubbing his Asian eyes with the hollow of his palms. Even though he is African American, I definitely got my daddy's eyes. His face lit up when he gained enough focus to make out my figure. *It doesn't matter how many times he sees me throughout the day his face always lits up like he just saw me for the first time. He is always glad to see me, even if he'll never spread his arms for a hug*, I thought to myself.

Glory's favorite cartoon was playing on the TV, and in no time she jumped on the bed, bouncing up and down on the spring. "You will stop that Glory, grandpa is trying to relax," I said. My mom was by now in the room and didn't have the kind of patience I had. "Get out of this room," she shot at my niece, and Glory stomped out with her head bowed. "She doesn't have to leave the room now does she?" my dad mouthed, and my mom shot back at him "Shut up dummy." I was still trying to understand what called for that when I heard Glory second my mom and said, "Yeah, dummy." I was thrown back, but that was just the beginning, as my mom continued to call my dad names with Glory repeating after her. My mom never corrected Glory and although my niece loves her grandad she can't help but be disrespectful when she sees grandma doing it.

Again, I never really understood how they managed to stay together for over thirty years with the way they go about talking to one another, as me, Glory, and my mom left the room. I sat on the couch and stared at the four walls. I thought about how much my mom hates me; she believes my dad treats me preferentially, but I don't let it get to me. They have their issues, and I couldn't be held responsible for any of them. Glory lifted my bag again, and my mom shouted at her to leave it be. "Listen to grandma, Glory Monroe Kennedy," I said to my niece, watching my mom roll her eyes at me. She hated it when I called my niece by her full name. My sister named my niece's middle name after me and refused to include my mom's name which made my mom despise me more.

"I have an idea and it's better than your play," my mom smirked. My mom has a million and one ideas and has never followed through with any. It was obvious she was fishing for a fight. You can always count on her to start an argument, but I refused to give it to her, especially not in front of my niece once again. So, I said as nicely as I could, "Sounds good, what is your idea?"

"You may be able to help me, I just designed some new greeting cards, but I have to get them copyrighted and trademarked. I don't want anyone stealing my ideas," she answered. "But of course mother."

"Where are we going, Aunty Roe?" Glory asked blinking her eyes. Her eyes were full of light, as I remembered we have somewhere to go. She was excited, and I wasn't going to let her down. "You tell me sugar, where do you want to go?" Glory loved the playground in the neighborhood; I had taken her there a couple of times, and she had been asking that we go there again. I was sure she was going to say, the playground. But I was totally surprised when she blurted, "Ice Cream. Let's get ice cream!" We grabbed Glory's jacket, as my mom said, "You are not going without me!" *Just great*, I thought to myself. We got ice cream and ended up at the playground.

* * * * *

It was my plan, I had been nursing it for a while, to tell my dad about Jay-O, but it was totally impossible to do so with the drama my mom put up the last time I visited them. I was grateful in a way though, because aside from the fact that Jay-O was good looking, I hadn't seen much to like about him just yet. We had gone on a few more dates, but he hasn't been too willing, or should I say available? He excused himself mostly with work. He acquired his second outlet in the city which according to him demanded more of his time now. I understood him, but I wanted more of his time. On the bright side though, his new outlet was just a stone throw from the studio where Jason - my friend come partner worked, so, it wasn't all that bad. Plus, I was quite occupied myself. I had this play I was working on, alongside my occasional photo shoots to get me out of my sabbatical, but then, I still wished I could see Jay-O more than I did in April.

Chapter 3 - MAY

It was no secret I wanted to spend more time with Jay-O. I wanted him more in my life. Trust me, I tried to control my wish to be around him, it just didn't work much. The bulk of our communication in April was done on the phone or through text messages. His texts were sweet. I'd be an ingrate to deny that. He loved when I sent him pictures or responded with the words, 'Yum' or 'cha cha cha' or if he said, 'You are beautiful' and I said, 'I know.' He sent a picture of me sketched by him. I was amazed as I was surprised. I never knew that part of Jay-O. He never mentioned he was an artist. There was no difference between me and what he sketched. I looked at the picture first thing in the morning from the day he sent it, and one morning, after staring endlessly till my eyes were sore, I made him a good morning video. He loved it, and I was pleased.

Speaking of good morning messages, Jay-O never failed to send me a good morning and good night text, even when he was in Boston visiting his gay friend. I thought it was strange though - a gay friend, but I never asked unnecessary questions, so I don't make him uncomfortable around me.

When he returned home, he kept inviting me to places that sounded great, for instance; Circus Soleil, paint while drinking, and a place where you can race in a Lamborghini, but we never actually went. The back and forth texting were fun and I was loving it, but it soon was going to lose its intrigue if we didn't see each other once in a while. I received another text from him saying, his parents are in town for Mother's Day, and I was so stupid to think he was going to introduce me to them. What was I thinking? All I got were their group photos, and I managed to pretend to be excited about seeing the pictures. I even made a video with the images, and he liked it.

In the meantime, I listen to the song, *Nothing Can Break us Apart* almost every day with confidence and finally he asked me out on another date. During one of our dinner dates he apologized for not being able to see each other sooner. He told me on top of work he also goes home to see his family on the weekends. I understood because I use to do the same thing when I lived in New York City. Needless to say, I told him I did not notice he was busy since I was busy too.

One afternoon, Jay-O took a picture of us and sent a text to his ex-girlfriends. I thought it was unnecessary. One of them sent a question mark as a response, but I made sure I didn't pry. We went out almost every day closing down each restaurant, literally going through at least three waitresses. He was drunk as a skunk. I wondered how he drove home. We had great conversations though, and he insisted on paying for every dinner and movie, not that he had a choice since I did not have a steady pay check. Speaking of which, he was concerned about me not having health insurance. I assured him I have insurance, but he wasn't convinced. He wondered how, since I don't have a job. I explained how I went to the emergency room when I wasn't feeling well, and they asked if I needed health insurance and I agreed to it. He smiled, and said, "Pretty girls like you live in a bubble." Whatever that meant, as we moved on to another conversation about my nationality.

"I have a little bit of everything. My cat eyes make most people think I'm of Asian descent, which is not true, my predecessors were Indian on my mom's side, so I tell people I have Indian in my family," I said. He chuckled. "My dad is Black but for some reason, he has the cat eyes." I continued. He seemed to be fascinated by my story. He went on to ask about my age yet again, probably because the waiter carded me, but not him. He was a bit upset for not being carded. I told him the same thing I did the first time he asked, "It's classified." I knew that I wouldn't be able to stall for much longer, as he was getting more agitated by the day.

* * * * *

Everything seems innocent and sweet and although Jay-O is a nice guy, I haven't had much luck with men; they start from being loving, awesome guys to huge jerks in a few months, so, I have my reservations, but I have my fingers crossed in Jay-O's case. On the other hand, I have been hurt and used too many times before. So I told myself I'm only going out on these dates with Jay-O so that I can get out of the house. One might think it's selfish of me, but I had to look out for myself. If I let the calls, dates, and messages get to me, it might be too upsetting when they eventually stop unexpectedly. It seems a bit pessimistic, but a little caution hasn't hurt anyone yet now, has it? Inversely, Kelvin and I lasted for about seven months and the ones before no more than four months. Why? Because as soon as trouble hits I leave, but I made a pact, however, to not give up so quickly on my next relationship.

The next day, Jay-O and I spoke on the phone, and we gossiped about his gay friend and his boyfriend. Jay-O loved to gossip with me. He loved my perception on things, especially because I was never judgemental of people and their decisions. During our conversation, I learnt about Jay-O's deafness in one ear, and I had to speak a little louder. I wondered why he'd kept straining to listen to me all this time, but I was as sensitive as I could be, lest I make him regret telling me.

We went out the next day for a stroll downtown. He told me about a bachelor party he has to attend next month in Brazil, and how he'll be going with his friend from his hometown. I thought this trip was too early in our relationship but it's not my place to tell him not to go. I noticed something odd when walking down the street near his store - no one spoke to him when he said, 'Hi.' It was like he was invisible.

We yakked more about him being a vegetarian. Since he is a vegetarian Jay-O's favorite food is French fries. So, one evening, he took me to one of his regular French fries spots, and we ate fully loaded fries with wine. He called some friends of his who lived in the neighborhood to see if they'd love to join us, but they were unavailable. One of them was a lady, and he passed a very silly comment, "She is the type of girl I'd like to marry." I didn't know what to make of it, so I let it slide.

* * * * *

Tuesdays were my busiest days. Jason was busy every other day of the week except for Tuesdays and Fridays, so we had our rehearsals and deliberation on my upcoming play on these days. The play was looking good so far, even though Jason felt there was much more work to be done because the play is expected to relaunch my almost dead career back to the consciousness of people. "I will speak with the breakdown writers; I think something is missing in the story; I can't quite lay my finger on it," Jason was saying. I was sitting not too far from him in a reclining chair. I could hear Jason's voice from a distance as if he was speaking from a crowd. My mind had wandered far. I was thinking about my first date with Jay-O after our meeting at the pub. Jay-O had been so shy that night. All he did was stare at me, and smile whenever I spoke until I saved the date of course.

"Are you even listening to me at all Monroe?" that was Jason, he was standing over me now, waving his right palm across my face. I had been staring into nothingness all along, and his voice had drowned into space. I jerked forward, stuttering as I assured Jason I was totally with him. It was useless though; even a blind person could see how distracted I was, as I continued to replay the memories of my first date with Jay-O. "I wanna go get something to eat, you want anything?" he asked as he headed for the door. "Nothing" I called after him, once again drifting back into deep thoughts. Now, I was thinking about Jay-O deafness in one ear. I believe that it's a good thing he felt comfortable enough to tell me about it, even though it worried me a little.

* * * * *

Well, the month ended. We got to see each other a quite a bit, even though nothing new or special happened. Jay-O still hasn't touched me, and now I'm wondering when he actually will.

Chapter 4 – JUNE

My mom had managed to suspect or maybe sense there was someone in my life now, even though I'm not so sure one can put it that way if all you do with that someone is text, and hangout without really touching or talking about making it official. She had mentioned it twice last month, because she saw me giggle on my phone when I visited them, and I had mentioned the name "Jay-O" on impulse more than once. I dismissed her on both occasions, but there was no holding off my mom on anything she's keen on. I wanted to wait to be sure of where the whole thing was heading before bragging about it to anyone. But, eventually, I had to tell her something this month, just to get her off my case. Not long after I told my mom about Jay-O.

Things began to look up and it seemed like things was getting more exciting. We didn't want to go on one of our regular dinner dates, so we went bowling and it was at the bowling alley one Thursday evening when we had a long awaited kiss. I'm inclined to believe that famous line that says, 'Good things come to those who wait,' because Jay-O turned out to be an excellent kisser, and there is no doubt the wait was worth it after all. I was still basking in the euphoria of the kiss the next night when we went out for dinner, and this is when he officially asked me to be his girl. It took plenty of determination to hide my elation.

Damn, was I glad! I thought that would never happen, and as if the excitement wasn't enough already, he invited me that night to his condo for the first time. I was almost angry he hadn't invited me to such a lovely place earlier. Although his place was as messy as my mom's and wasn't furnished well, the condo itself was so lovely, and like he had mentioned before he enjoyed a view of the harbor. We spent the rest of the night kissing; before asking him to take me home.

That was just to be the first of many visits to Jay-O's fine condominium. I became a regular guest. Jay-O always insisted I took off my shoes at the entrance; it was some sort of OCD I guess, but it was all right with me. I was at his place one night, drinking a bottle of my favorite wine he bought for me from the winery downstairs in his building. He also ordered food with a dish that included a steak for me and vegetables and rice for him. How wonderful. We watched his favorite movie, *Twilight,* but all we ended up doing was kissing and breathing into each other's mouths. He wouldn't take me home, and I was happy to spend the night.

I asked him to sleep on the couch. He had a look on his face like he didn't expect me not to allow him to sleep in bed with me. He agreed though; and attempted to sleep on the couch, but five-minutes later he was at the bedroom door with a sinister look on his face that made me feel uncomfortable. I inquired what was wrong and he expressed how displeased he was with sleeping on the couch. He eventually slept next to me till we both fell to sleep.

Staying the night at Jay-O's became a habit, and we would sleep in the same bed without having sex, and he never let me see him entirely naked, it was pleasant, to say the least. All we did was make out, and it was great.

* * * * *

Ironically, it thundered-stormed every night I stayed, as my beautiful blue journal fell out of my hands, and it took time to locate the page I was writing on. I found it eventually, but I had lost vibe by then, so I looked up our Chinese signs. It said Jay-O is an Ox, and I a dragon. According to the readings, this makes us the worst match, as we will argue every day. I quickly consoled myself with the fact that I'm a Christian, and Jay-O is a sweet guy. I hated myself for reading it in the first place and I continued to write in my diary about Jay-O and me.

* * * * *

I was spending so much time with Jay-O now, and even he began to slack at his work, missing his morning shifts not arriving until 3 o'clock in the afternoon. Luckily by now he had trained his managers well enough to take care of his business pretty well. One of his managers was getting suspicious so Jay-O said he would tell him he is taking real estate classes, but instead he made sure he went to the store in the morning like he use to do.

Jay-O was gradually loosening up. By the way, he looked at me; I could tell he adored me and we were inseparable. Also, he was no longer the gentleman I once knew, and he had become so naughty and expressive. We even gave each other hickeys like we were back in high school and as our romanced deepen, one morning, he confessed to me, with eyes heavy, and sober, that he loved me from the top of my head to the soles of my feet and that he couldn't live without me, but I took it as an expression triggered by some rush of emotions. So, I ignored it, lest I got my hopes too high. Instead, we watched a movie which had a marriage scene in it and when the couple said their vows, it felt like we were saying it too. It was such an awkward moment. Speaking of awkward, Jay-O farted, and it was obvious he struggled to muffle the sound without success, I didn't say a word though, but it was awkward.

He showed me his smoking side too, which I was totally fine with, and I decided to tell him I'm celibate. After Kelvin, this is what I said I wanted to practice until I got married, but Jay-O didn't seem to hear me, or he intentionally ignored it, I'm not so sure.

* * * * *

"How do you feel about wearing short hair," Jay-O asked one day as we sat at a basketball court taking in fresh air one evening, and I told him how I once had short hair all through my modelling years, and how I got tired of it and preferred my hair long.

* * * * *

We had passed the time for hiding and seek now, we had become very popular in the precinct, and we went everywhere together. I briefly met his employees, Vivian the owner of The Playhouse next door, and he met my grandmother officially. I could even hear people chatter good things about us in the neighborhood and so I didn't really pay any mind to the few people who warned me to be careful so I won't get hurt. "Didn't I just see you with a blonde one day and then a brunette the day after," a resident from across the street said to Jay-O. He laughed. According to one of the residents, Jay-O is a flirt, and he would kiss his female customers whenever they won a free TV from the store during giveaways till his aunt asked him to stop the practice, but then, isn't that what people do? They gossip, just to ruin a good thing, as they joked on us about our hickeys making the senior ladies from my grandmother's building a little jealous. I chuckled.

A lot happened this month as I remember. Jay-O took his trip to Brazil with his friend. Although I was a little disappointed he did not ask me to babysit his condo or car while he was gone...well, who am I kidding we just met. He did invite me to go with him to Brazil, but I needed him to know I trust him. He gave me no reason not to. As an alternative, I talked my cousin's ear off asking him did he think it was too early for Jay-O to attend a bachelor party. He said I was worrying too much. Besides Jay-O was still really excited about me.

When he returned, I jokily asked him if he had sex. He had a surprised look on his face until we laughed. He did admit he met one Victoria lady, and he wouldn't stop talking about her, it unnerved me. I said one night during his gloating about her, "I'm glad you are opening up about this girl instead of me finding text messages from her, that's what women get upset about." But by then, I was getting curious about who she was. He even told me they had a very good time together, which of course he claimed to be innocent, but I almost lost my temper when he told me she cried when he was leaving. I couldn't understand why he would tell me that. He wouldn't stop mentioning and bringing her up; it was almost like he enjoyed saying her name or something.

He continued saying, "She stayed at the house in Brazil where all the guys stayed and she cooked breakfast for everyone. I even promised to help her daughter speak English." I was sick of listening to him go on and on about her. "Jay-O, whatever happened between you two should stay in Brazil and not be brought back here to our relationship," I shot back at him as calmly as I could without letting my anger show. He obediently agreed and said, "I showed her pictures of you, babe." I trusted him and I could tell the girl was looking for means to get herself and her daughter out of Brazil so she would not have to prostitute herself anymore and she needed a nice guy with money in doing so. She was not going to trick my man, even though he is a little naïve.

Then again, I suggested an open relationship arrangement to him, but he refused, to my satisfaction I must say, and as expected we kept getting closer. We even shared experiences of past relationships. I told him about Kelvin and the reasons why I haven't been in another relationship since. "We grew apart, me and Kelvin," I said, making sure not too bad mouth my ex-boyfriend to him. "Other than the four girlfriends you had before me, when was your last long term relationship?" I continued. He said he was in a two-year relationship that his family and friends disapproved of, so eventually, he cheated on her. "Although my ex is Asian, we followed the same religion, and she came from a good family my aunt broke us up because they did not think she was the right one for me," he said. *Your aunt broke you guys up?* I thought to myself. "She loved me, so since she lives in DC I suggested she come to my place to stay for a week to see if we could work things out but it went sour. But she still wanted to stay with me and even allowed me to cheat, can you imagine that? But eventually we split up." I listened keenly, taking mental notes. His ex-girlfriend seemed too desperate. I would never allow him to cheat on me.

We talked more about our careers too, me a college graduate, and him a college drop out. In its place he shadowed several store owners before his family allowed him to run the electronic store himself. Speaking of which, I asked more about his family and he proceeded to tell me his family is very strict and that his mother and aunt are crazy and annoying people but he has a favorite great aunt who comes to visit from Paris from time to time. And even though he and his brother did not grow up with their parents it was like they did because his aunt reports back to her sister about everything including their relationships.

We continued to talk about my career and from some of his questions, I could tell he was stalking my website. I thought that was cute, and come to find out he loves Lenny Kravitz. I told him I met him a few times and he was impressed.These things were probably meant to bring more assurance, but I couldn't help but feel that our relationship won't last. "I give this relationship until August," I told him. He smirked. You couldn't blame me anyway. Jay-O wasn't convincing enough. He ran out to take calls on our dates, he even answered an unexpected call that came in at 3:30 am when I spent the night, he still kept a bag of clothes of his ex which I made him dispose of, and whenever I said nice things about him, he was quick to correct me about him not being so nice. One of his remarks he mumbled, "You'll see**.**" He also said he was in-like with me. *What happened to him saying he loved me?* I thought to myself. Not to mention, Jay-O seemed to plan every move in advance. He told me he was to leave to go to his hometown for two weeks in August, for an event at his temple. *Leaving again?* I thought to myself, but August was still about a month away, he was only giving me a heads up.

Looking on the bright side, I haven't been this happy in a long time and even the thought of losing Jay-O scares me. I don't want to even think about it for fear it may jinx things. I'm acting ridiculously superstitious, I know, but I can't seem to help it. I really love him.

Altogether, the month was quite an eventful one. We bonded just as I wanted, and despite what our Chinese signs said, so far, we had yet to have any major quarrel, and that was pretty cool. This lead me to believe that Jay-O would past my ultimate test and that is we will be together on July 4th. There is no way he is that type of guy who would start an argument so he can hang with his friends and then try to and get back with me after the holiday. We have had three great months together. And not to mention his birthday is coming up right after July 4th.

The only thing that went wrong this month was that I had to find another venue for my play since Jason pronounced his place unavailable.

Chapter 5 - JULY

My guard was down to a considerable low. I had unknowingly began to do the things I never thought I would do, and I hated myself for it. Jay-O and I were moseying along the waterfront stopping by one of the bars one evening, the moon was full, and we were talking politics amongst other things, and our conversation drifted to entertainment and celebrities. I think I must have been a little tipsier than I realized, because for the first time, I spoke about my previous flings with a few celebrities. It wasn't hard to tell it made Jay-O jealous. It was such a cute sight, watching his eyes grow wide and bulgy in their sockets. He wanted to know who the celebs were in particular, but I wasn't going to divulge that information. That led to our first major argument. Jay-O would have preferred I never mentioned it at all, to my holding back on their names, as our bartender walked by and Jay-O yelled he needed a drink. I wondered why he was ardent on knowing them. I told him eventually, and it all just made me feel like an open book. In my eyes, Jay-O was knowing too much, and I couldn't even hold my tongue.

Our PDA game had become so strong too. There was no place where we couldn't touch each other and kiss. It was intriguing. We were having lunch and drinking wine, getting tipsy and kissing each other so shamelessly. Jay-O's right palm was on one of my breasts, my leg was stretched across his lap, and we sipped wine at intervals as we kissed and touched. A guy came in with a woman, heading straight for our table with his eyes wide with surprise. I wondered who they were. The guy looked quite surprised to see Jay-O in such a situation as we were when they walked in. "How are you doing, man?" the guy asked Jay-O. "I'm good," Jay-O answered. "Meet my girlfriend," the guy said, and Jay-O shook hands with her, right before he introduced me as his friend. Oh, I was furious. I felt like a cheap slut. *How could he introduce me as his friend? especially considering we were all over each other*, I thought to myself. I contained my disgust but not for long. As soon as his friend left, I asked him why he introduced me as a friend. "He's my customer, I can't let him know about us just yet," he said. His response aggravated my anger more. I couldn't place it, none of it made any sense. I created a scene and dashed to the ladies room to collect myself. I returned and Jay-O already paid the check. It goes without saying that we didn't close down that restaurant, what more, Jay-O broke up with me before the night ended…a day before July 4th.

Shock cannot begin to describe what I felt when Jay-O said it was over between us. Just like that. He dropped me off at home, and zoomed off as though he was running away from the troubles in his life that threatened to kill him. Needless to say, the scale has tipped and he was no longer my night and shiny armor…no longer my care bear and this very affectionate whirlwind romance came crashing down. A stimulating relationship ending before it got started.

I cried myself to sleep that night, and the night after that, and the night after that, and the nights that followed for the rest of the week and instead of me singing *Nothing Can Break Us Apart*, I was singing *Lost Ones* by Lauryn Hill.

* * * * *

The set date for my play kept drawing near and I was writing additional scenes as new ideas popped in my head. I went through the manuscript every day even if I had nothing new to add. But today was a little harder than normal because Jay-O was on my mind, and I struggled to keep my line of thought undivert, but it was close to impossible. And on top of that, Amber, my prodigy, who was supposed to perform my play kept expressing her doubts and fears. It was to be her first performance, but I had given her more than enough training and my confidence. The change of venue didn't help issues though, as she had grown comfortable around Jason's place where we were meant to use initially and where she had all her rehearsals. I had found another venue - *The Center*, but she failed to identify with the huge stage. Jason had suggested before that I was supposed to perform the role myself, and I eventually did. The play was a success, and I even got a congratulatory message from Jay-O on social media.

* * * * *

I was at the park with Glory and my mom. Mom and I were discussing Jay-O, and Glory was at my feet snuggling and cuddling my leg like a cat. I thought it was annoying, but mom said it's normal for children to do that, as they need the warmth and affection from loved ones. So I let her be, as mom and I kept on with our chit-chat. She did wonder why I was so hooked on a guy I just met and why I had a hard time finding the right man. I wondered too, but it was funny that I was hanging out with my mom, but I had to give it to her, she was amazing and compassionate when I needed her after Jay-O broke up with me. It was the first time in ages that my mom was genuinely nice to me, but I have to be careful with that because a couple of days later she will throw everything I told her in my face and tell me it's my fault Jay-O broke it off.

I also can't forget my mom is the one who broke up my sister's family by calling child services to have my niece removed from their home. This is why my niece lives with my mom and dad now. My mom did it for selfish reasons and that was to stop my dad from divorcing her and she needs my niece's check. She knows my dad loves my niece and would not leave her while taking care of my niece. She use to whisper in my niece's ear when she was an infant to call her mommy. Sick. But she got what she wanted. It devastated my sister and on top of that, my mom constantly tries to ruin my relationship with my niece, but she and I share a bond that no one can break. A bond I thought I found in Jay-O. My niece shows me what love is and I refuse to accept less, therefore; I never want to see Jay-O again.

But anyway, I loved hanging out with my mom and Glory since my break up with Jay-O and now that the play is over I was not sure what I will do. I can admit that is one thing I do have in common with my mom. I have great ideas but I cease to follow through with any of them. But I do know this, I don't want to go back thinking about Jay-O, even though he kept bombarding me with text messages all through the month, especially on his birthday. The old Monroe would have given in and responded, but I stood my ground. Wow, my biggest fear that he would dump me before the holiday and then try to get back together before his birthday was playing out in reality, and although I said I never want to see Jay-O again, I changed my mind, yes I did, I'm a woman and I can change my mind. With that said, I decided to make him suffer from the silent treatment for a full month, though I feared I would compromise if I became idle; therefore; I joined an online dating website; but I could not wrap my head around dating online. So, I continued to spend time with my family instead, and it felt good. Meanwhile, we moved to a quiet Jewish neighborhood and that helped me out greatly to forget about some of the memories Jay-O and I shared together.

Jay-O texted and texted saying he was sorry and regretted his actions, but I sure wasn't going to let him off that easy. He had a lot to answer for, breaking off the relationship baselessly was one, his reluctance to introduce me as his girl was another. He had to understand how much he messed up, and I didn't think he had yet.

Chapter 6 - AUGUST

I was waiting by the doorman for too long. He kept making up flimsy excuses. "Please ma'am, you can't go up now, I have to wait for Mr. Jingguo Lee's go ahead." That sounded ridiculous, "What go ahead? Don't you know me? Am I a stranger here?" I was venting, I hated embarrassments like that. Since when did Jay-O have to give the go ahead before I could go up to his apartment? and he was home; that was what vexed me more. "You are not one of those crazy ones are you?" the doorman said. "Ha ha," I replied. When I was eventually allowed to go up to Jay-O's apartment, I was exhausted. The plan was to talk things over, but I wasn't sure I had the motivation to do so anymore, and when I got to his condo, what I saw devastated me more. He was with a woman. It was the same girl he had told me he met in Brazil some time ago. My head felt light, and my legs wobbled. Jay-O wasn't remorseful, in fact, he told me to leave. I was heading out in tears, when I woke up in my bed, covered in sweat and quivering. My heart was thumping fit to burst out of my chest. My Jay-O! Oh, it was all but a dream. What a relief. I looked around for my phone to check the time, it said 5:35 am. I couldn't wait for the day to break. It was time to end this. I had to see Jay-O and sort things out before I run totally loco.

I was at Jay-O's place before 8:00 am, and to my disappointment, he had travelled to his hometown. We spoke on the phone, and he promised to head back the next day. I felt relieved, to say the least. Jay-O returned the next day as promised, and we met in front of my grandmother's place. He was looking so unkempt. His hair had grown out of place, and he had gained weight. We took a walk, and we spent the whole time bickering and arguing about who was right and not. He even claimed he never broke up with me and that he was alone on his birthday. I figured out how delusional one had to be not to know that he did something of such significance, but it was almost impossible.

Jay-O was sad I missed his birthday and demanded a gift. He said I missed an important birthday because he was now out of his twenties. *I hope he knows now not to play anymore games with me*, I thought to myself. We got back together, and I spent the night at his place, and the next night, and the night after that and now he was demanding sex and I could tell he was becoming frustrated with the celibacy clause as it became clearer that it wasn't a joke after all.

* * * * *

Jay-O was packing to travel again for a religious function he spoke to me about at the end of June. I did not like it one bit since we were supposed to be bonding considering we had just settled. "You know,

I was thinking, why don't you go with me on this trip baby?" That was Jay-O wooing me into accompanying him on his journey, but I declined, for reasons that are yet to be clear to me. As a substitute, we texted and talked on the phone, and he explained his religion to me. I told him I'm a Christian and that I devote my time to prayers in the morning and church on Sundays. He did not agree with my religion nor did he respect it.

When he got back, I asked him if he had sex. As usual, we laughed. I stayed a few nights at his place, still without sex. He was getting more and more irritated. At first he was such a gentlemen and now I was waiting for what would be his next plan of action in regards to my celibacy. I feared things might go horribly wrong, especially because this is normally the point when I have to break it off with guys who pressure me for sex before I get married. And although I gave in with my other relationships I was determined to stay true to what I believe. I guess you could call it being a reborn virgin, but for real, I felt like I was waiting patiently like a vulture waits for its prey to die before devouring it.

Chapter 7 – SEPTEMBER

Labor Day was fast approaching, and much to my dismay Jay-O wasn't going to be around. He has a wedding to attend in his hometown, and for some lame reason, I wasn't invited. First July 4th and now this? *I wondered why he invited me to a wedding in Paris, but not in his hometown?* I thought to myself. We argued over it, but it didn't get anywhere, so I ventured off to the Hamptons on a friend's invitation for the Labor Day weekend. We had a ball, and I made sure to post the pictures on my social network page so that Jay-O could see I was having a good time without him. It worked too because he was calling, but I refused to answer his calls. When I talked to him the next day, it turned out that he had come back just in time to be with me on Labor Day. I didn't regret my action, though; and refused to reveal who I went to visit in the Hampton's.

* * * * *

There was trouble in paradise. A lot of unsettling things were coming to light. Jay-O was adamant about me cutting my hair short, and now he wants a cat? I ignored him. He almost even nagged about it. We quarrelled a lot now, mostly on Saturdays. I spent my Wednesdays through Saturday at his condo; that is of course before he starts a flimsy argument that leads to a break up by Saturday evening. I suspected he had another woman he entertained from Sundays to Tuesdays, but when I confronted him, he put an end to the trend.

I came back to his place to meet a condom wrapper in his bedroom right beside his bed. Jay-O was in the bathroom, and the five-minutes it took him to come out to face my confrontation seemed like ten years. I was swollen and ready to explode like a time bomb by then. I queried him about it, a little violently I must add, and he explained how he used it to jerk off to avoid making a mess. It almost felt like a jab aimed at me to make me see how wrong it was that I hadn't allowed him to have sex with me. It was hard to believe, but he sure made it sound credibly believable, and if he was lying, it must be a running joke amongst him and his friends.

The same incident repeated itself, and the following day I saw another condom. I could not believe that he was using it for what he claimed he was using it for, so I approached him again to see if he'll give me the same story and he did, but this time, he had a lot of attitude, his reason being that it is embarrassing to discuss. I left it alone, and from that day I never asked when I saw an opened condom wrapper in his bedroom. Not that I didn't want to, or it didn't drive me mad, but I tried as much as possible to avoid altercations.

* * * * *

One day on the phone, he says you have crazy eyes. I asked what that meant, but no answer. Then he told me about a story his customer told him just the other day. He said one of his friends has a daughter who cried rape when she had relations with her boyfriend. Jay-O asked me what I consider rape. I was speechless.

Ironically, we had sex for the first time the following day after so much booze and making out. His touches were so perfect and impossible to turn away. During relations, he had a sinister look about him that turned me on even more. I totally lost it when he spread my legs apart and ate my clit like a major course. My ecstasy knew no limit, I gave in and watched him slide his rod into my already slippery wet womanhood. I stopped him five-minutes after, and he was furious I didn't let him climax. It continued like that for a while, even though I wanted so badly to be celibate. I never let him go past five-minutes, though. He insisted I used prophylactic pills, but I never did. He was clearly afraid of getting me pregnant.

I got my greatest disappointment when I asked him about marriage, and he said he never wanted to get married, a statement I know so well to be handy when you have no intentions of walking down the aisle with someone.

* * * * *

I detected a change in Jay-O. He was no longer shy or sweet; instead, he told me he is an asshole, arrogant, and has a big ego. He said he used to be insecure but not anymore. He even had the nerve to say, "We are past August," as if our relationship was a challenge for him. You would think I would run the other way, but there is no way this guy is all the bad he says he is. We continued to go on dinner dates but not closing them down so much as we used to, and then, eventually that dreadful question came up that I didn't think was important to him. He asked what I was going to do with my life. I was thrown back by the question. I hadn't taken the time to think about this since the play, but one thing is for sure, my mind is always working, and I always have new ideas. Conversely, from the look on Jay-O's face as he smoked and coughed while I struggled to answer the question, I knew mere ideas wouldn't suffice, and I'll have to pick a career soon.

His cough was becoming incessant, and it worried me. Not that I hadn't noted it before, but it was obviously a concern now. I asked him about it, more so to divert his attention from the subject at hand, and he said it's a smoker's cough. Jay-O showed me his smoking side not too long ago, but I did not realize he had a slight habit. He smoked first thing in the morning, right after work, and before bedtime.

Some days, I stayed at his place while he worked. He would come home and see everything cleaned and most days his food cooked. He would never say thank you, but instead, he found something wrong or looked for the next thing for me to do. "Why did you move my food around in my refrigerator?" he said, slamming the refrigerator door and marching to his room. *On the contrary, I specifically made sure I placed everything in the same spot after cleaning his filthy refrigerator?* I thought to myself. His neighbor had to say to Jay-O one night in passing that he saw me make two trips to the recycle bin during the day. "This one is a keeper," the neighbor concluded. I just wish Jay-O will appreciate me that much.

That evening, after having done too much during the day, I drunk some wine to relax. I was totally oblivious that my period was due. The flow was heavier than usual, and in no time, my head felt light. "Jay-O, call 911!" I managed to say, with the little strength I had left in me. He called for help, but by the time they arrived with an ambulance, I was feeling better, and they were ordered to leave, but not before asking me personal questions, for instance, am I pregnant and what is my age? Jay-O politely left when they asked my age. Needless to say, Jay-O and I laughed after the EMT left. I said, "You see too much."

Sometimes, I made a joke about him eating me out like it was his first meal. I said, "For you to be a vegetarian you sure like to go downtown." He responded, "I said I eat fish." We laughed hysterically till we both got pains in the pits of our tummies. I loved it when we made silly jokes. Another thing I like is his height. I have to admit I loved Jay-O's height. A waiter once complimented us on our height and that we looked good as a couple. I love to lay down on his bed and look up at him when he left the bedroom. Not to mention the several tattoos related to his religion and his beads that slept around his neck - they represented his religion. He looked so yum.

The next morning, I asked him for money to have my nails done. I had the money, but something about being pampered feels so sexy to women. The response I got though was not in any way sexy. "Don't go asking me for things like I'm your sugar daddy, and mind you, you did not get me anything for my birthday, and yes, I've not forgotten, and neither am I letting it slide." "Well maybe you can cook your own dinner," I blurted, and I made up my mind never to ask him again. But he certainly did not have a problem asking for $200 to put towards his mortgage.

* * * * *

I finally spent some time with Vivian. She was too loud and talkative for my liking, but she was incredibly funny. Surprisingly, she calls him Jay-O too. *See I was not the only one who misunderstood the pronunciation of his name*, I thought to myself. I do remember Vivian from back in the day during my modeling days, but she played as if she did not recognize me. I played along. And come to find out she was the one who assured Jay-O that I was going to come back to him after our fallout during the summer. I struggled to understand why she was all up in our business.

* * * * *

Jay-O asked me about the hug I gave him when we first met in the pub. He wondered if I hug everyone else like that. The statement was probably meant to be funny, but it ruined the moment. I don't know why he had to ruin the moment with such silly talk. It was totally uncalled for. I retaliated, and I said, "That was a friendly hug because I knew how shy you were, so I figured that would break the ice, and bring you out of your shell." I got the desired effect, as his countenance changed immediately.

* * * * *

"Baby, have you ever considered beefing up security around your store? I know this is the city of brotherly love and you are in a nice neighborhood, but then the next couple of blocks from the store could be trouble. A little safety could be nice. A gun maybe. What do you think?" I said. "I hate guns; I can't stand them at all. I do the best I can security wise with my golf club," we laughed simultaneously. "I turn off the cameras and wham! Besides, we haven't had many cases of robbery or burglary, except when my employees steal from me, but eventually I fire them." I understood his reasons, and so I nodded, as I traced out a tattoo on his back with my index finger, watching him jerk as it tickled him.

I was to wait for him at the store one day so that we could head to his place together. I waited on end, and when I was tired of waiting I visited my grandma's, a few minutes later, Jay-O called and said he was ready, and that I join him outside. I sashayed out of the building, only to see him coming out of Vivian's playhouse. It was quite unsettling, but I wasn't going to allow it to lead to a fight.

We headed to his place, as I thought about my to-do list. I knew I had to use his laptop system when I got to his place, as mine was damaged. Once we arrived, I pulled out my flash drive and inserted it. Jay-O had a huge kick out of my flash drive, saying I'm old fashioned to still use a flash drive. He pulled it out of the system, and it ended up damaging the stick with all the information I had stored on it, but at least, I had a back-up in Dropbox.

I downloaded the documents I needed to his desktop and that's when I found something displeasing. I saw pictures of a girl with short hair on his desktop. I ignored it and used the laptop. The next day I asked him if he could leave his laptop while he was at the store, and he agreed. While I was using it, I saw messages from other girls. One that stood out the most was a girl named Cindy. He was flirting and asking her to meet him at one of his store locations. The message ended, so I did not know what happened after that. I said nothing to him about it.

A week later, after having non-climax sex, he went to the bathroom to take a shower. He left his phone on the bed opened. I was surprised because lately he sits in the bathroom with his phone doing who knows what while the water runs. I stared and then out of curiosity I checked his phone, I saw messages from girls from a dating app. I asked him about it and he said they were just friends, I didn't buy it, and it led to a break up. We eventually got back together, and to worsen it all, he called me by the name of Lisa on my first visit after making up, and he denied it, saying I was crazy and delusional. Jay-O's misgivings and transgressions were piling by the day, and I religiously ignored them all. It wasn't easy, but I had no choice if I wanted to remain at peace.

We went out to dinner one evening after he kept me waiting while he was in Vivian's playhouse doing whatever he does there. Everything was going smoothly, till he excused himself to use the gents. I asked to use his phone, and while I was on a call, a call kept coming in from Terica. Terica is certainly a girl's name, but funny how I was ready to accept this Terica is a man if it had to come to that, but her photo was displaying on the screen too. She was dressed in super-hot lingerie. When I asked Jay-O, he elucidated she was just a friend who writes plays as well, and she's married. It goes without saying that we split again. He dropped me off at my grandmother's, and he kept calling my grandma's till I accepted to make-up with him.

* * * * *

I haven't mentioned Jay-O's bad sense of style. He hardly ever knew what to wear, as opposed to me who always looks smashing like a model, whether we were going on a date, or just taking a walk. But I liked when he dressed like a surfer boy. We were strolling on the deck near the water one afternoon, feeding the ducks. During our stroll, a video chat came in from Jay-O's mom. He picked up and I heard him tell his mom he was at the store. I felt it was unnecessary to tell such lie, and figured, if he could lie like that to his mother, I knew he had no problems lying to me. He excused his action after the call, saying simply as he said before, "My mom is crazy, you never know with her." I smiled and nodded, I totally understood him, but he had yet to know I had a crazy mom too.

Jay-O kept going on and on about my employment status, and how he wanted me to find a job. I had it in mind already to find one, so I can have some income while pursuing my passion, but the way Jay-O was going about it really upset me, as he bragged about how great his business is and that he is worth $600,000 if he was to sell his condo and business today and how I have nothing. Needless to say, the conversation drove us to the verge of yet another break-up and a few days later making up again. Sometimes I think that my pact to stick by my man was not a good one to have with Jay-O. I figured he is younger than I am and needed time to adjust and figure out what he wants from this relationship, but I resolved to ask God if Jay-O is the right man for me before making any drastic decision. The first time I asked, I would see something from Jay-O's store that reminded me of him. I asked again a week later, and when I opened my eyes from prayer, I saw something else from his store. The third time I asked, Jay-O's picture popped up on my phone. So, I guess he is the right one for me, so I'm never asking again.

Jay-O eventually asked me to work the cash register in front of the store. I did for a little while, but I hated it and thought it was dangerous. I told him I'd prefer to do the office work. That lasted for just a short while too, because he always found something wrong in everything I did. He was never satisfied. He fussed over everything, and I gradually began to find he isn't the nice guy I thought him to be. And to my surprise, Jay-O's manager has been telling him I only want him for his money, and this is why Jay-O has been acting shady. He listens to what other people say, which is quite unhealthy for any relationship. I was disappointed because I thought he was at least grown enough to know this. I told Jay-O, his manager wishes I was his and not yours.

* * * * *

Eventually, I told Jay-O I had to stop having sex with him whether he climaxed or not in five-minutes. It drove him crazy, but I could no longer go against my beliefs. We broke up after that of course and Jay-O drove me home. During the ride home, Jay-O drove with one knee while he texted almost the whole way there. I reviled it but I didn't say anything since I was busy wondering if he was doing it to get me angry, or he wanted us both dead. On the other hand, the drive was boring, as we were both mute and the car felt like a graveyard. Then, out of nowhere, Jay-O blurted, "Can you love me the way I need you to?" but I didn't as much as make a peep. I had enough. It's not like we hadn't had sex. I couldn't understand what else he wanted. I felt he is disrespecting me and my values, and if he didn't want me after I told him I was celibate, he should have left me alone when we first spoke about it.

He marched me to the front door of my parent's place and from the look on his face, I knew we were going to make-up. We did. He threw me in the corner of my parent's building and grabbed me. I could feel his fingers pressing into my flesh. My heart was rapidly pounding. My body was on fire as he spun me around lifting my skirt. I melted into his arms. "Monroe!" I heard through my parent's door. We abruptly stopped and bade each other goodbye, with the promise of seeing each other the next day.

* * * * *

When I visited Jay-O at home, I noticed bathing after work was like a religion. Even on weekends when he didn't stay too long there, he showered when he came back home. Speaking of weekends, I loathed when he worked on weekends. Jay-O told me he used to fuck customers at work before he met me. It was clear from the way he said it that ladies throw themselves at him especially on the weekends when women were off work or out of school. I didn't let that faze me. He's with me now.

Jay-O continues to buy me wine each time I went to his place. Very expensive wines I may add. He never allowed me to pick a cheap wine. He thought it is undermining, but I didn't care about the price of a bottle of wine, as long as it calmed my nerves and got me relaxed. But sometimes the wine got me too relaxed, enough to let my guard down and allow him to have sex with me again. I'm not sure though, if he keeps buying me wine because he found out the effect on me.

* * * * *

Jay-O loved to watch football. He will make nachos, drink beer, and have French fries whenever he watched a game. Most times I had to clean up whichever mess he made. He kept his condo and his car so messy, and he needed new furniture. All attributes that continues to remind me of my mom. I could clean the mess though, but I wasn't going to do anything about his furniture. Usually, I will be glad to change it from my pocket, but not after he'd hinted he can't marry me. On top of that, Jay-O and I argued, fought, and broke-up a lot, and it was disquieting, especially because we were only about three months old, excluding July, and those early months are the honeymoon of relationships. If you asked me, I'll say we haven't entirely recovered from the July 4th misunderstanding.

* * * * *

When Jay-O went to his temple on Sundays, I always wondered if that's what he was really doing. To me, Jay-O did not strike me as a serious enough person to go to temple all day long. Moreover, I had enough reason not to trust him. One day, the girl he boasted of as "the type of girl I would want to marry" texted him while we were lying in bed, and said herself and her son were in the area and wanted to know if Jay-O could give her a ride home. He didn't feel like it, so he told her his car is in the shop. I thought it was rude, but I was glad too that he didn't go. But I hope to meet this girl soon to see what's so special about her.

I observed too that Jay-O had a locked photo app that he wouldn't allow me to see. It upsets me whenever I remember it, but I left it alone, as my butt hit the flat screen TV in his room one afternoon and it fell to the ground. I feared it got broken, but it didn't. It came on minutes later after plugging it back in the wall. Jay-O was far away in the kitchen, so he didn't know what happened. All he heard was the sound, and he shouted to ask if I was ok.

* * * * *

Sometimes I wondered where and who are Jay-O's friends, as I've never had a chance to meet any of them, but I decided to ask at a perfect time. But I did ask him about his bad ear out of concern over the phone when he called to say 'good morning,' he denied ever claiming to be deaf in one ear. *Uh?* I thought to myself, but I left it alone.

* * * * *

We were no longer the celebrity couple we used to be, but I couldn't help but notice he'd become popular in the area. People chit-chat with him now, rather than before when it seemed like he was invisible. I'm not one to blow my trumpets, but it's clear I had upgraded him. It had become cool to have a conversation with him, as he's dating a hot model now.

One day while at his place we got into a discussion about my ethnic background yet again, and I said I got Indian in my family jokingly. He asked that I stop saying that because I sound stupid. It was out of context, rude, and unnecessary to say that to me. I didn't let it get to me. "Okay, so I got Asian in my family," I replied. "Ha, ha," he said sarcastically.

* * * * *

I am spending my days at the store these days. Helping Jay-O out or keeping him company when I'm less busy or idle. I thought he enjoyed that until one day he said, to my consternation, "You know you sat here for eight hours not doing anything." I figured it was too rough and rude, till I began to realize that he has a lot of employee drama and he runs his place very unprofessionally. Some employees even complain about not getting paid. When I asked him about it, he said they are lying and he doesn't give a fuck what they say because they steal from him and the African American employees are never on time and they don't work well, and that he likes to work with Spanish people. Funny how the Spanish say he takes their money too. One day he showed me an example by making me watch a Black employee wipe down the counter, and how much better the Spanish one wiped down the counter like he enjoys it. I concluded Jay-O is crazy and hard to deal with.

While we were at his store Vivian stopped by being loud as usual to pick up Jay-O's car key. I asked, "Why is she here picking up your key?" He then explained why he lets her use his car since he uses her parking space for free. I couldn't help but notice his closeness with Vivian. She either stops at his store for a chat, or he went to hers. It seemed like they were flirting, but I didn't want to sound like a jealous girlfriend or make a fuss out of mere suspicions, so I said nothing about it.

* * * * *

I had to re-touch my hair one night and he asked me to come over the same night. He washed it for me and it felt so good. But I could not resist saying one of my favorite lines now, "You see too much."

* * * * *

"I don't know what kind of friend you are Roe. You could go for months without hearing from me, and you'd be fine. I can't. If I didn't know better, I'd say you didn't love me," That was Penelope my bestie. She called very late one night, complaining about how bad I am at keeping in touch. I was guilty of all she accused me of, and I knew it. So I just kept mute, and let her vent. "I'm sorry Penny. You know I love you. I'm just very bad at keeping in touch, plus there's been so much going on with me lately," I said after she was done ranting. "What's up girl, what's been happening?" she asked, her voice suddenly bright and enthusiastic. More than anything, Penelope loved to get the gist and catch up. Sometimes I believe she refuses to call me in a while so she can listen to all the gossip that must've piled up over time. I told her about my play, then about Jay-O, and everything that had happened with us. Penny isn't one to take a half or incomplete gist; you had to give her a lowdown, and since she was the one who called, I gave her all the gist. She was okay with the fact that he owned a business of his own, though her tone hinted that she didn't think too highly of the kind of business it was, contrary to Jay-O's claim that he has the best business ever. I wish he knew how wrong he is.

* * * * *

Jay-O will later tell me why else he sometimes acts shady with me. He told me he lost trust in women since his high school girlfriend slept with his then best friend. *How worse could it get?* I asked myself. I remember Kelvin saying something similar to me when we first met and now I am yet with another guy who is holding on to what a girl did in the past. It takes years, if not decades for men to recover from such things as heartbreaks. That's why they treat women like dirt, but I focus on the times Jay-O can be really sweet. Like when we cup or hold hands, and just recently, I got sick and he nursed me back to health. That was a lot to handle, and it must've taken some commitment, because really, I was a horrible mess, and so I appreciate his care, but like I said before, he sees too much.

* * * * *

Jay-O had his way of ruining things and making our affair go sour. He introduced me as his friend again on a date. We argued about it, but I didn't have the energy or mental strength to fight.

* * * * *

I have a funny feeling, or maybe a hunch, and I hope it is just that. Jay-O got off the phone with his brother sometime after talking for over an hour. I thought it was a family matter they discussed, but apparently, his brother was telling him about how he just broke off a relationship of two years with his girl. I remembered immediately that Jay-O's last relationship lasted only two years too, and I couldn't help but think there was a pattern. Like the brothers had some kind of pact or two-year limit. It's silly, but like I said, it's just a funny feeling, nothing more.

The "funny" feeling overwhelmed me, and eventually I couldn't help but express my fear to Jay-O. He found it funny and got a huge kick out of it. He laughed at me till his eyes were teary and said, "Babe, you think way too much. A two-year limit, really? Who does that?" I just sat mute, feeling awkward. I shouldn't have mentioned it or entertained the silly thought in the first place. He debunked the hunch, and then told me about how his aunt will always say that any girl he dates should live with him for six months just to see if she can put up with his crap. "Your aunt is right about that," I said jokingly, but it seemed to dent his ego, so I apologize, and kissed him on the forehead. He touched me, and then kissed me back, but not on my head. He kissed my ear. It tickled, and he knew, as he enjoyed watching me cringe. He kept planting kisses everywhere, and I lost my will power with each kiss.

Jay-O yanked off my tank top in one swift move that seemed like magic, exposing my robust tanned breasts, and he began to suck on my nipples, making them tighten and grow taut. I was aroused in no time. Jay-O knew how to stimulate me through my nipples. The things his tongue does cannot be explained. I was weak with pleasure and watched him strip me of all my clothing. Jay-O spread my legs wide apart, knelt down before me, and squeezed his tongue into my already wet, and steamy cunt, and with the ambidextrous tip of his tongue, he licked the insides of my womanhood from wall to wall till his tongue got soaked with my juice. I was dripping wet and running like a fountain. My head was thrown back, as I held his head down with one hand and dug into the skin of his back with the other. I was lightheaded but didn't want him to stop. He kept at it for minutes, before getting up to kiss my mouth again so I could have a taste of my cunt on his lips. I was panting by then, and almost out of breath. We made love, and it was mind blowing as I climaxed and squirted all over the bed.

Jay-O was more than happy. I could see the feeling of fulfilment in his eyes. "Wow, I never knew you were a squirter," he said, and I buried my face in the pillow. I was too shy to look at him. September ended well, amidst all the drama. The sex seemed to make it all go away, and we both felt new, as our bond strengthened.

Chapter 8 - OCTOBER

September ended on a high note for us amidst the whole problems we went through and while I had my reservations already, I was still hopeful that things might change for the better. So as time went on, I noticed he spent more of his free time chatting on his mobile phone and when I challenged him, he went "Why don't you get yourself a real phone and move with the world baby girl," but I just smiled and did not make a meal of it. *Though I felt if he really wanted me to get a phone, then he could get it for me and make the payments, after all, he did that for his aunt, brother, and uncle,* I thought to myself.

Gradually, he began to be free with me and open up more; it was almost as if the shyness had evaporated. I accompanied him on his weed purchases and it became so frequent that I was wondering how he had never been caught or even at the least quizzed by the police and as if reading my thoughts, he said, "Well, I see you're a little bothered about my weed pickup; trust me, it's no big deal because the police rarely give me trouble because I am Asian and my face looks so innocent plus I have passed by them several times without so much as a stop despite having quite a number of drugs in my car at different times." It was reaching a point of boasting and bragging for me, but before I could take a break from his rambling which was what it sounded like to me, he went on to tell me about how he indulges in hard drugs and blackouts from drinking so much with his friends whenever he goes to his hometown. *So my boyfriend smokes weed, drinks, and takes hard drugs and is proud of it, great!* This was the thought going through my mind and I began to wonder how long the relationship will last.

From accompanying him on his drug deals, the next thing I know is that I am being called funny names like nigga, slut, hoe jokingly and with a sense of humor, but it doesn't mean I enjoyed it. The only thing is that he knew nobody else would understand the use of such words or names, so he only said it around me. Instead of saying something about it, it was around this time I came up with phrases like "You know what," "Now you see that," "You better stop calling me names," "Have you lost your mind," "Imma bang you in your face," " You better stop calling me nigga." But among them all, my favorite is "You know what," and the purpose of these phrases was to keep me from saying what's really on my mind because I was not ready to bicker or argue unnecessarily.

* * * * *

Being a Christian that I am, I realized I was not living my life as I ought to especially with Jay-O and who can blame me, I mean have you seen this guy? So I ensured I had my morning devotions regularly to ask for forgiveness of my sins. But like I said, it's hard for me to stay away from Jay-O. One night, we went to a Nepalese restaurant and while eating, there was light music; the night felt so perfect and ambient. I had the urge to maximize it so I told him that we should dance. We got up together, his arms was around my waist with mine on his shoulders, we moved our bodies slowly to the light music and against each other…It was really a moment to enjoy and dare I say, one of our finest moments.

* * * * *

I came to realize one thing about Jay-O and it's the fact that he feels he's better than African American people; like African American people don't have much to give or even say in regards to their neighborhood or environment which to me felt shallow; *I guess he's been around the wrong Black people*, I thought to myself.

* * * * *

By now, I put the play to the side and now I'm into organizing modeling workshops and sales of my books and as usual, Jay-O continued his faithful showers throughout the day, keeping his car a mess, and smoking whenever I am at his place. Moreover, Jay-O's real nature in a manner of speaking began to surface as he was sanctimonious about everything like talking down to me like I am a child. He will say stuff like "Why are you using the same rag you wipe the counter with to wash the dishes. Why do you have the fork on the counter and not on a plate? Use a potato peeler, not a knife; that's not how you load a dishwasher." I adjusted but then sometimes I would take my finger and poke his butt hole while he was bent over in the refrigerator which would make him a little mad but was funny to me.

One day, we were lying together on the bed and we were generally schmoozing when he said, "I know I invited you to go to the wedding in Paris in a couple of weeks baby and as much as I would have loved for you to go with me, I can't afford it right now. But on the bright side, I got you something." And then he went into his bag and brought out a lingerie with pink color, my favorite. He came back beside me on the bed and I couldn't help but admire the lingerie, and as if reading my thoughts, he said, "I am sure this will look sexy on you and I hope you will wear it for me when I come back from my trip." I just smiled and blushed as he said it, but I was still disappointed about not going to Paris with him and I wondered why he would tell me this at the last minute.

* * * * *

Vivian was once again back in the picture and Jay-O always had one excuse or the other to see or spend time with her. When it was time for him to go home, instead of going through the alley, he would go through her store to get to his car. He claims he did not want to be robbed while he had cash in his backpack.

But rather than be insecure about it, I continued to be the good girlfriend making the bed in the morning and washing his clothes while I fix him a breakfast of a bagel with cream cheese or a croissant with cheese and coffee. As time went on, he began to see my love for chick peas and parsley. I loved pizza too.

* * * * *

There is this friend of mine named Martin who sends me texts and tells me nice things about myself; he likes me and he wants to marry me but I wasn't interested in marrying him. One night while in Jay-O's condo, I was lying down on his chest and then he pulled my hair back and said, ''I just wish you will listen to me and cut your hair short,'' to which I gave him a stern look and told him that I love my hair long and if he loves me, then he should let my hair be and with that he dropped the matter. Some few minutes later, Martin called and we talked for some minutes as he made me smile and laugh all the while Jay-O pretending to be asleep but what do I care?

Before going on his trip, he was a little bit indecisive as to whether he should go or not. Finally, he left on the Monday of the third week in October but before leaving he carried out some actions that left me fuming. First, he told me I cannot stay at his condo while he was away and secondly he gave his car to Vivian to use and not me, I mean it was unbelievable and I was aghast. When I confronted him about it, he was all, "Well, Vivian has money and can pay for any damage to my car but you, baby, you don't have any money, so you see why you cannot have access to my car." *He actually speaks like he is broke*, I thought to myself, but anyway, this made me mad but I managed to calm myself down and did not make a big fuss about it. He then went on to say, "When I return I will put you on my car insurance." That made me feel better but I thought it was still mean to allow Vivian to use the car more so than his girlfriend.

When he left, I visited my friend Martin in New Jersey and spent a few days with him. While I was there, Jay-O called to check up on me, but I didn't tell him where I was. It was during this period that Jay-O's cousin grabbed the phone and was ranting, "Hey, listen, you better not be breaking my cousin's heart or I'm gonna shove my fist down your throat." I didn't even utter a word because I was not dating her and she obviously has no idea of how her cousin was treating me.

* * * * *

After getting back from the trip to Paris, he told me about how he travelled to London with his brother and how his brother met a girl there. Unmoved by what he told me, I asked him my usual trick question of, "Did you have sex over there?" and as usual, we laughed.

* * * * *

His hair began to grow long which I thought was sexy but what I did not think was sexy was that it seemed like we were breaking up every other day and then working it out again. We would start out nicely and then end ugly… seemed like we were beginning to develop a pattern and for some reason, we could not completely leave each other. On another note, I began to meet some of his friends, Danny who was older than him gave him good advice, and then Phil who is a fanatic Christian. "The world is coming to an end. Make sure you remove your money from the bank and buy plenty of water and food," he said, and then ask Jay-O for $20 as if Jay-O owed him the money for that information. Jay-O would grin and call him an idiot.

* * * * *

Jay-O being a guy with a bit of an ego and a boastful personality took the time to explain to me the level of wealth that his aunt and uncle has, that in fact, he and his brother were born into it, but his family had to work hard to become rich. "I had an audit today and I'm $8,000 in a hole," he said to his aunt on the phone one day. She sent the money to him the next day with no questions asked. Not that I cared, but Jay-O still made it a point to let me know. Although Jay-O is rich he is still a little bit scared of being poor like his uncle and aunt use to be so he never stops working and he researches other ways to earn money. *This is why I guess he acts like he is so poor all the time*, I thought to myself.

* * * * *

After some busy time at work, Jay-O showered, hung out in the bathroom with his phone and running water, and then he made time for me. We both relaxed and watched a movie while I would fall to sleep in his lap. Then as if woken up from slumber, he said, ''Hey baby, why not put on that lingerie I bought you,'' and like a woman whose sexual side had just been aroused, I smiled and got up to go and change. By the time I reappeared, I was clad in the pink lingerie he bought me, *Damn! Don't I look sexy?* was the thought going through my mind. Jay-O could not hide his excitement. ''You look incredibly sexy baby and the lingerie looks exceptional on you.''

Like a young teenage girl just finding love, I giggled and who could blame me, it's been a while Jay-O said something nice to me. He moved closer and kissed me and for the first time, he was really gentle with me nibbling at every part of my skin that was exposed beginning with my neck all the way down. My body felt different; gradually he peeled the lingerie off my chest and took my breasts in his mouth and sucked on them before moving to paradise and inserting his rod into me. He pounded until I reached orgasm but he did not stop until he released and the way his body vibrated would be just like the movement of a train.

We were both exhausted, he pulled me closer and kissed me on the forehead and said, ''Do I feel defeated?'' but I chose not to answer him because it seems apart of his big ego, he knows how to ruin good moments.

After some minutes, he picked up his phone and was texting with 'the kind of girl he would want to marry.' Come to find out her name is Mallory and he is in a group chat with her and five other chicks. He complains about removing his name from the group because all they conversant about are their kids.

* * * * *

We are now at a point where we bang often, either for five-minutes or we go all the way and have make-up sex after a break-up, and now, he removes his beads before having sex because one day, a part touched my sugar pack and he acted weird like he had committed sacrilege. I was left speechless once again because a lot of things I had done with him were against my beliefs. Speaking of body parts, he began to emphasize on me wearing a bra. "I have small ones. I don't need a bra," I responded.

Thus October ended and a certain pattern had been established in my relationship with Jay-O, I was still hoping things might change for the better as time goes on.

Chapter 9 - NOVEMBER

We continued doing the nasty and even though it was against my beliefs, I was getting better at it and the sex itself was more enjoyable because my actions during sex were like that of a pro and I can tell Jay-O liked it. He also liked that the playoffs for football was drawing near and we watched most of the games together, and of course, he had his beer, nachos, French fries, and pizza and wine for me.

One day, a friend named Hung came in from out of town to watch the game and Jay-O and he was so happy to see each other; it was obvious they really like each other but at the same time, his friend was facing the same problem I deal with - Jay-O's arrogance and telling his friend to get a job which was why despite the likeness, there was also some distance between them. They were not as close as they ought to be. For me though, I was glad to finally meet one of his friends from his hometown and I later discovered he was the one that Jay-O went to Brazil with.

Although I met his friend he refused to introduce me to his family. Around the second week of the month, his aunt and uncle visited from out of town and met him at the store, but he would not let me meet them. He told me they would not understand our relationship. They would not understand why I don't have a job and they want him to marry an Asian girl. I said a few things that was inappropriate about his family and he cussed at me about it and demanded I did not come to the store. When his family arrived at the store I had to wait for my grandmother while he went to the store to meet his family; he just left me on the bench hanging. I felt so used and it was impolite for him to treat me like that. But Vivian made sure she was at the store. She knows them very well. I heard that his aunt asked who I am and Vivian was like, "I don't know who she is, but she is hot!"

* * * * *

He asked me my age again and I still gave him the same reply as before and that is my age is classified and that I'm 19 forever. But he insisted, saying that his aunt is wondering who I am to him and asking questions he doesn't have an answer to. So, finally, I told him and he was shocked.

* * * * *

One thing about Jay-O is that he rarely forgets things and he made it a constant reminder to ask me for his birthday gift but I just shrugged it off. And as usual, my boyfriend still hassles me about getting a job saying it's better for me to find a steady job with a retirement at my age rather than still chasing my dream. *This is why I hate telling people my age. They beg me to tell them and then they judge me,* I thought to myself. However, I did agree with him although I hate when I feel pressured. On the other hand, I'll rather focus on my entertainment career rather than listen to someone dictating my life to me; someone who doesn't care enough about me or deems me good enough for him to marry. So, I was going to look for a job at my pace and time. But he continued to emphasize on me getting a job. "I don't like my job. Nobody likes their job. But I go into my store every morning even though I'm worth $600,000 if I sold everything today, you have nothing." *He loves to tell me how much he is worth. Besides, doesn't he know that $600,000 is not enough money these days, but I don't want to burst his bubble like he does to me,* I thought to myself.

Once again I explained to him my situation but I realize that Jay-O has no clue about sacrificing and struggling to get what you want so I said, "Hey darling, do you realize how blessed you are with this condo and store which has allowed you to live a comfortable life; I guess you are grateful for having your uncle and your aunt in your life," and his next reaction was to take offense because he felt I was talking like his uncle and aunt just handed it to him just like other people had been saying. He believes that he would still have all of this and in his defense, claiming that he had other investors interested. But the truth is there is nothing like having your family as an investor. I mean you can't call an external investor and ask for $8,000 and have it in the bank the next day with no questions asked.

Anyway, my wonderful boyfriend argued that he worked hard before they gave him the store and that he had been employed at other electronic stores while at the same time ensuring he paid his aunt and uncle back, so, therefore; he is not dependent on his family. But he was missing the point which is that he is blessed and not a lot of people get the opportunities he has. And despite all his efforts, ironically, he is dependent on his aunt and uncle while his brother is not. In fact, when it comes to the issues of their family, Jay-O and his brother are contrasting in character.

* * * * *

Vivian continued to stop in his store constantly or he goes to her store if she doesn't. They were getting too close for liking. It was as if now that she sees him with somebody she wanted him. Her guy friends even began to ask questions, but she just waves it off by saying he is a friend. I would ask the same question except her boyfriends would end up leaving her alone. They both agreed that they have a friendship pact and if the person they are dating doesn't like it, well they don't care. Needless to say, it was now a constant source of argument; and then he asks why I am so worried about her and he said, "I didn't even like Vivian at first. She is loud and fat, but my aunt said I need to cope with her because she is a business woman and I may need her for business advice or something." The reason was not so bad except that they were not that close before and now they can't do without seeing each other, quite profound! In fact, she still comes to borrow his car quite often. To me, this girl is moving in on my man and he is too stupid to see it or he likes it.

* * * * *

In the next few days, Jay-O would tell me he is going to Las Vegas in February for a business trip and would like me to come along. I thought it was perfect since Valentine's Day was at the same time we were leaving. In the meantime, I took a trip myself to New York City to visit a friend and I came back with a phone with service my friend gave me. Jay-O was happy I finally got a phone.

* * * * *

On my birthday, he took me to watch a movie and then we went for dinner afterward and that's where another fight started. He was angry again that I was not putting on a bra and then he went on to say I refused to wear a bra because I was seeking for attention. ''Why don't we go and see Mallory?'' Jay-O said to me. With a puzzled look on my face, I said, "Why?" *Well, I would like to meet 'this kind of girl he would like to marry,'* I thought to myself. I was a little tipsy and still curious, so I continued, ''Yes let's go to say hi.''

So, we went to see Mallory who happened to work at a lingerie store, yeah I know go figure right? I met her and she was not bad but had a different look than I expected. We chatted with the girl and out of nowhere, he said he wanted to buy a bra for me. So she picked one out and off we went to the dressing room together while he waited outside. After confirming the fitting, we paid and said our goodbyes.

On the way to his house in the car, he asked me, "How was it in the dressing with Mallory?" He then proceeded to tell me he could not stop thinking about us in the dressing room while he was waiting outside. I laughed and told him I would never tell but then I asked him, "Why is Mallory a girl you would want to marry?" "I don't know. I mean, she is really good with her child and stuff...look, I don't know why I said that. Mallory said it was stupid for me to have said that to you," Jay-O answered. So, I said, "Wait a minute, she knows you said that to me and yet you introduced her to me. I thought it was something you said to me? So now she knows she is the type of girl you would marry? I mean, why tell her that?" All of a sudden he blew up, spit came out of his mouth, and he banged his dashboard. And said to drop it. I have never seen him like this. He was so mad. I cried and cried and cried and he turned the car around so he could drop me off at my grandmother's place. He cussed me out the whole way there; I was dumbfounded and embarrassed, I mean, all of this on my birthday? But for some reason I cannot explain, we ended up calming down and we went back to his house and made love. Maybe I was over reacting.

* * * * *

Thanksgiving has arrived. His aunt and uncle left out of the country as they did every year according to Jay-O. He and his brother normally stayed behind and made overloaded French fries. This year is different simply because Jay-O and his brother are in relationships. His brother had dinner in DC with his new girlfriend and I made Thanksgiving dinner for Jay-O right here in Philly. *This is my first time ever cooking Thanksgiving dinner. I hope Jay-O loves it*, I thought to myself. But I have to admit, sending him to the store to get the ingredients was my first mistake because he did not bring everything back. The second mistake was when Jay-O told his aunt which ingredients I needed while he was on the phone with her. She convinced him we had what we needed in the cabinet. I ended up using the wrong spice for my macaroni cheese, but it still came out great according to Jay-O. We had an awesome Thanksgiving!

* * * * *

Jay-O had an unusual request for me. He asked me to look into a storage building around the corner from his store. His good friend Danny use to own it but he had to let it go. However, his plan was to buy it again but Jay-O wanted to buy it from under him. He would do whatever it takes and uttered, "I guess I will have to burn a bridge to get it."

Chapter 10 – DECEMBER

December began just like any other month with Jay-O continuing in his normal habits like the taking off his faithful showers, smoking weed, and wanting sex from me and I still drink my wine. The employee from the liquor store asked Jay-O why he buys the wine all the time. *Hater*, I thought to myself. Of course, this started an argument between Jay-O and me.

I began to observe more that Jay-O has a bad temper. He gets mad at a drop of a hat. I mean, he's so angry that sometimes, he tells me he wants to die. I then reply to him and said, "You have everything and all you say is you want to die?" But on the other hand, maybe it has something to do with his parents not being there for he and his brother when they were growing up or even now. He is the only one here. But it's still no excuse to treat people badly especially me. He would yell at me at his place, in the car, and even at his business. It got so bad one day his customers could hear everything. He is still yet to drop the whole gift for his birthday saga. Anyhow, we went back to only having five-minutes of sex with no climax. I mean I could not keep going all the way with this guy I'm not married to or who has no plans on getting married.

* * * * *

Jay-O still goes home on weekends leaving me behind. Okay, so he does not want to introduce me to his family yet but I can still come with him and hang out.

He claims he does not have money to spend on dinners and hotels. I told him I have friends in DC and we don't have to spend a lot on food. He declined. And when he leaves guess who gets the car. Vivian.

* * * * *

I searched and searched for employment and finally I got a job at a small hotel. He got upset because I turned down a job where I would make a couple of more dollars with a bigger hotel. He finds something to argue about all the time. I told him I don't want to be in the hospitality business I just want something laid back so I can pursue my dreams. The other job was going to have me too busy. Besides, I don't plan on working at this job forever. I have a degree and I plan to use it in a few months along with pursuing my dreams. But it doesn't matter where I work because he always seems to find something to make a fuss about. Even when I cook, he complains about how I prepare food and wonders how I am still alive if this is the way I prepare the food I eat. We cannot get through a day without an argument just like my mom and I.

* * * * *

There was a day that I got sick again and the way he treated me was as if I had a communicable disease like leprosy or something, in fact, he wanted me to leave under the guise that he didn't want to be sick. He ended up pulling out a spare bed to sleep in. I guess the days of special treatment are over since he had sex with me.

* * * * *

I started my new job at the hotel part time. It is a couple of blocks from Jay-O's store. *The girl I work with is hot. I don't want Jay-O to see her*, I thought to myself. At any rate, I did not mention that my boyfriend owns a store right down the street in fear I would get the question, "So, if your boyfriend owns a store then why are you working here?" I wanted my independence but at the same time, I knew Jay-O was cheap and now I'm thinking spoiled.

While working I discussed my boyfriend problems with my aunt and she kept telling me that the relationship was all wrong for me. I know it is but for some reason I cannot get rid of him and even when I try he keeps calling and calling until I pick up the phone and we finally get back together. I also discussed my boyfriend issues with my grandmother and my mom. They both suggested I leave him alone. I even told my dad and he helped me get through issues from a man's point of view. His advice helped for a little while.

* * * * *

I had dinner with Martin one day and he gave me a birthday gift. Turned out to be a laptop. I was so surprised. But I wondered why my friend had to get me something I need but not my boyfriend as the same with the phone.

So finally, I gave in and got Jay-O a birthday gift on Christmas day even though he doesn't celebrate Christmas but I did not have the heart not to have anything for him. He, in turn, handed me some balled up wrapping paper and inside it was a $100 pre-paid visa card.

* * * * *

He still hates that I'm working at the smaller hotel and that I'm only working twice a week. He said some horrible things to me, making me cry so hard. It seems to me I had to tell him more about my background. Even after I told him about my history and how I did not think it would be this hard to transition from modelling to the real world and how I wanted to kill myself at one point but God saved me and gave me hope. Yet, that did not change anything as he still jabbered at me like a dog. I told him my family and friends understand because they know my history and the struggles I have been through. They knew me when I was at the peak of my modelling career making tons of money and when I lost it all. I told him there is no one new in my life because they would not understand my situation. But because I thought he was a nice guy and doing his own thing he would be okay with all of this and that's why I got close to him. But I was wrong. He is the most arrogant person I know. Now I see why his aunt said, 'live with your girlfriend for six months to see if she can put up with your crap.'

Again, he says he knows he has an ego and he is an asshole. I never cried like that in front of a guy before. I use to tell myself if a guy ever made me cry and I cried in front of him I would leave him. But I am making Jay-O an exception and I don't know why.

He and I traveled that oh too familiar road again of having full on sex but I had stopped it again and explained to him I'm a Christian and I don't believe in premarital sex. I know in his heart he thinks I want to trap him but he fails to realize I said I want to have sex after I get married. I did not say I want to have to sex after I get married to him. Get over yourself. Whoever I get married too I want him to have my vajayjay. Of course, he ignored me and we had our five-minute sex instead of the full on sex. He said, "So is Jesus hanging out in the closet watching us when we have sex? Tell Jesus to get out of the closet."

Jay-O then began to bother me about why I only cook sometimes and not every day for him and then I apologized and made some stir fry and a batch of his favorite cookies. I promised to do even more in the hope that it will stifle our fights and arguments. But I was wrong; he still found something wrong with everything I did.

* * * * *

At a point he wanted Vivian and I to be friends and so he forced me to go shopping with her one day using his car. He offered me money, but I declined to show my independence and not seem like a gold digger I guess. "Goodness this car is a mess, but I'm just glad he lets me use it," Vivian said. The way Vivian was driving was shocking to me as if she was high on drugs or something but I held my peace and focused on being a good girlfriend. But what stunned me, even more, is when we arrived at the store and I found something I wanted to buy. I said, "Dag I should have taken the money Jay-O offered." Vivian replied, "Girl you should have taken the money. You have to know how to train a man." *I guess she thinks she has my man trained, uh? If he only knew this girl is using him but hey he is using her too. Friends? Please*, I thought to myself.

Going to the store with Vivian did not appease my thoughts towards her. She needs to respect my relationship and that's the bottom line. However, no matter how I try, he keeps complaining, and now out of nowhere, he had something to say about his car not being clean. "Why don't you clean my car?" Funny how he had something to say after Vivian made her remark about his messy car. Honestly, I thought he liked it messy. Anyway, I cleaned his car, no I take that back, I took it to the car wash and purchased the detailed package. Jay-O told me how stupid I was to spend money on an old car. He only wanted the inside clean not the outside, but it didn't matter. By the next day, the inside of the car was dirty again, just like I thought. He likes it dirty.

THE BREAKUP

We are good together when we are not arguing; we have so much fun and these are the kind of moments I wish would not end but if wishes were horses, beggars would ride. So the year came to an end and on New Year's Eve, we were at his place, drinking and watching a movie before falling to sleep. Ten minutes to the New Year, I woke up and vigorously shook Jay-O for the countdown but…

Chapter 11 – Happy New Year!

New Year's countdowns should be fun, but Jay-O managed to drain the countdown of all its fun due to his slumber. He never listens. I had warned him earlier to slow down on the booze, but "I got this," was what he kept replying. Watching him lying on the floor with his mouth half opened as he slept while others were wishing each other a happy new year was depressing, so I said to his unconscious body, "You really got this, don't you?" I couldn't complain though. We were together, and that was all that mattered. It was the first time in the past few years that I will be with a man of my own on New Year's Eve. Jay-O woke up the next morning - the first day of the year, full of apologies for his inability to wake up for the countdown. "Baby, I was so tired. I don't know what hit me," he said. "I warned you to take it easy with the booze. You start the year with an apology; I hope this doesn't mean you'll keep offending me all year round," I teased.

As much as I hate working at his store, I was left with no choice than to lend a helping hand on New Year's Day as all of his staff were on break. I wondered where the customers came from. It was the first day of the year, people are expected to be home with their families. I watched Jay-O lie to the customer's one after the other as they asked how he spent the eve, telling them we had a good time and all. However, there was this one persistent man. He wouldn't buy Jay-O's lie. He called Jay-O a jerk after he made him confess he slept all through the countdown. We ended up having another argument before noon that day, about my not wanting to be in the store. I left eventually.

* * * * *

Jay-O complains about the birthday gift I gave him. He said the gift doesn't count because it was not on his birthday. *So, why did he keep bringing up the gift then? I tried to make things right whether he deserved it or not but he is still not happy. His customer is right, what a jerk*, I thought to myself.

* * * * *

"That's not a good sign at all Roe. He is telling you how the year is going to be," my aunt said after I told her how my New Year's Eve went with Jay-O, and I agreed with her, but wasn't going to let it trouble me. "He admits he is an asshole," I added. "I would not want to be with a guy who admits he's a butt hole," she laughed. Speaking with my aunt was always refreshing. She never judges, and her ideas are sound. "You know, he always sticks up for his family and fusses me out whenever I talk about them. He wouldn't even allow me to meet them, and I think I deserve to by now, regardless of my job situation or our cultural differences," I ranted, to her. She was with me on that too.

* * * * *

My work was taking more of my time now, and cooking every night was fast becoming a burden. I explained to Jay-O that I could only cook on Sundays and freeze food over the week, that is what I learnt from watching Martin's chef, but he wouldn't have any of that. He rebelled, comparing me with his aunt who loves to freeze food. I'm not even his wife, and I fail to see why I should have to worry about these things, especially when he's indicated that he has no plans to marry me.

* * * * *

I may be paranoid at times, but I'm quite observant. Jay-O's next door neighbor left him a note to come over to her house. He claimed she asked everyone on her floor for a get-together. My aunt says, "The only way this relationship is going to work is if you share him. He likes too many other women."

* * * * *

There was talk about me cutting my hair again, and this time I showed him a picture of myself with short hair. He preferred the long one of course - I look better with long hair. So he didn't mention it again, but I realized Vivian has a cat and keeps short hair and I guess that's why he wants me to have short hair and why he wants a cat. Jay-O could be very ridiculous. Just as he will sometimes say he doesn't want dinner, but when he gets home he's asking for his dinner. Leading to arguments. Of course, I end up making dinner on such occasions after he goes to his room with an attitude. I never thought I would say this, but he is making my ex-boyfriend look good. I keep telling myself I want to walk away but I don't want to give up on us. But some days I cannot take it, so I break up with him. Sometimes the reason was so stupid I forgot why. I just knew I needed a break. He counteracts by calling and texting. It's not fair because he doesn't give me time to get over him, so I end up right back with him.

Instead of dwelling on the bad I thought about the good in him and reminisced about the time we first met. "Babe, remember last year when we use to close down the restaurants laughing and talking." Come to find out he said he hated closing down the restaurants and having to pay for all of the dinners. I had no idea he was taking notes and tallied up dinners and then waiting for the day to throw it all in my face. I thought he was enjoying himself. Besides, he invited me to places and I did not need all of that. I was shocked and so was my aunt when I told her. Now I know why it took us two years to go out. It was a warning and I should have left him behind the counter at the electronic store. "I have an innocent face. I fool everyone with my dimples and beautiful eyes. That's one of the many reasons why I'm the favorite in my family. My brother hates it," he boasted, as he lifts up one eyebrow." He does that quite frequently.

* * * * *

We went back to having full on sex again. I don't know what kind of hold he has on me, especially since having sex does not keep the girls away. One Tuesday evening at a wholesale store, we came across this Chinese girl Jay-O knows from the temple. They exchanged greetings as expected, and to my disappointment, Jay-O yet again introduced me as his friend, and when I asked why, all he could say was he didn't want her telling his family he's dating outside the tribe. How preposterous. I use to always wonder what it would be like to date either an Asian or an Indian. To me they always came across as good men so when I met Jay-O I thought this was my chance to be with a real man. As far as Asian is concerned Jay-O has changed that belief. And it doesn't help that his weekend visits to DC became even more incessant, and he still hasn't offered to take me with him. I don't know what to think about these trips anymore, but I'm becoming quite suspicious. My aunt thinks he has another family and my bestie said he could be a drag queen. It sounds far-fetched but I remember when Jay-O tried on the bra he got me from Mallory's store and not to mention a portfolio I saw with dicks he drew. "Can you imagine what it's like having something shoved up your ass and then the feeling of it being pulled out," is what Jay-O said to me on the toilet taking a shit while I lied on the bed looking in.

* * * * *

Once again he was indecisive about going on yet another trip. This time to Las Vegas next month but he knew for sure he was not taking me now. He claims his friends are not bringing their significant others so why should he. I was furious but I asked will he be back in time for Valentine's Day and he insisted he would be. I left it at that.

* * * * *

He attempted to tell me something about one of his employees one day in the back of the store and when I responded he told me I don't have an inside voice. *Whatever*. Mallory and her boyfriend walked through the door. I pretended to be happy to see her. We conversed, but her main reason for their visit was to let Jay-O know that she and her boyfriend are getting married. Jay-O looked happy for Mallory, but I could tell secretly he wishes it was him.

* * * * *

"I really can't stand you being in the kitchen while I cook," I was saying to him one evening after we had several arguments about his non-stop fault finding in everything I do. It's almost like he is deliberately pissing me off. I ignored him of course. I have got to a point where I avoid arguments as much as possible no matter who's right, but I'm inclined to believe this is partly influenced by what his friend Danny said to

Jay-O one day. Apparently, he doesn't think I'm the right girl for him. There he goes again listening to what other people say.

But whether he is in the kitchen with me or not we fight endlessly and the fights are getting worst. I can't count how many times I marched down his hallway upset or placing my butt in his hallway chair bawling and minutes later he would come running to calm me down. I don't understand this guy. Neighbors could hear us screaming and slamming doors to the point where the condo association said we have to quiet down, bringing back flashbacks my mom and dad went through when my sister and I were growing up.

In addition, he constantly throws me out of his store and his home, sometimes at 11 pm with nowhere to go, leading to numerous break ups. When we break up, of course, he constantly calls and texts. Like I said before, the text always start out nice, apologetic, and forgiving but then if I don't answer his messages or get back with him he becomes evil. Eventually, throwing darts at me using his words and leading me to curse at him. I never cursed in my life until I met him! But somehow, someway, we make up. Still, my job has no idea what's going on and I like to keep it that way.

I always wondered why he didn't send flowers when he first saw me two years ago. I was only across the street at my grandmother's. Now I know why. Jay-O is not romantic. All he wants is sex and for me to cook and clean. I feel like his modern day slave. But he knows when to be nice to keep me around like finally putting me on his car insurance not knowing I had rules, unlike Vivian. Every time I use his car I have twenty minutes to get back no matter what I have to do. In the meantime, he is calling and calling and if I don't pick up he text. When he finally reaches me he argues and yells, "When will you be back?" "I just left," I said. *Vivian takes as long as she wants. One evening our day was over and we had to wait for her to return*, I thought to myself. I sped down the road at 80 miles per hour to return his car. It is not worth me using his beat up car.

"Why didn't you fill my car up with gas?" he said. *Vivian brings it back on empty. Are you serious?* I thought to myself. Of course, we argued, wondering why Vivian doesn't have a car of her own. She is supposed to be so successful. "Some of Vivian's customers fly in from Detroit and spends $5,000 at her store," he bragged. He consistently puts her on a pedal stool and puts me down. That is what really makes me upset, but he likes to get a rage out of me. I do wish he supported my ideas maybe I would be further along like Vivian. I'm sure she does not have a boyfriend around putting her down now or ever. Everything is always my fault. One day Vivian had the nerve to ask Jay-O why he doesn't help me with my business ideas since I'm his girl. She loves to seem like she is on my side and he loves to come back to tell me she is on my side. But I don't trust her and I wish she would keep her comments to herself. I also wish I had a parking space to offer him, so I can get away with at least half of the offenses Vivian does. I had no idea a parking space is so valuable.

But enough is enough, as soon as I dropped off the car at the store here comes Vivian dashing towards me to grab the car keys and stomps out the door. I couldn't keep quiet, so I hollered, "Are you his girlfriend too?"

* * * * *

"What are you getting me for my birthday baby?" Jay-O asked me as we promenaded down the street one evening. I actually hadn't thought about it till then. I smiled and told him to be patient as his birthday was still six months away. "I hope you don't pull the same stunt you pulled last year. It's another special birthday. I'm turning 30 and since you got me nothing last year this one better be a good one." "I did get you something," I reminded. It surprised me how that didn't turn into another argument; I was ready for one. It was a good thing we didn't argue though. It was okay to have a peaceful time for a change, specially, since some of our fights got so bad I ended up leaving out the front door while he was in the shower. I caught a cab to my grandma's. He texted and called over and over again. I thought my phone was going to crash. It serves him right.

* * * * *

Jay-O grew his hair so long into a ponytail, and at times people even complimented his hair than mine. To be honest, it looks so good on him.

* * * * *

I may not have met his family, but I'm meeting his friends from DC now. They come into town to visit Jay-O quite often. They all like me and I like them, particularly, his best friend Nick. Jay-O also is getting invited to a lot of weddings and bachelor parties overseas. He has not invited me to any of them, not even to his best friend's wedding in DC. He says he cannot get a plus one to the weddings and the bachelor parties are just for the guys. "You can't afford to take a trip with me even if I wanted to meet you there for a day or two before the bachelor party and I can't afford to buy you a plane ticket," he says. *There he goes being cheap again*, I thought to myself. But it really didn't matter because it got to the point where we could not plan a trip based on the fact we would be broken up by then.

He also complained a lot about having to pay so much money for his mortgage and it doesn't help that his store hasn't been doing so well, mainly because his employees steal from him. Again, I have never been around someone so rich be so cheap. But I guess that is how the rich stay rich. Speaking of which, Jay-O's plan is to inquiry about a roommate. "I want a roommate who does not eat meat because I'm strictly vegetarian now which means I don't eat fish anymore and I don't want you eating meat anymore at my place. I only allowed it because I was trying to fuck you," he said to me in one of his rants. His aunt put up an ad and a few weeks later Jay-O found a roommate just right for him, a vegetarian from China who surprised Jay-O by asking him about me.

"Babe you won't believe what my roommate asked," Jay-O says. "What is that hun?" I replied. "He asked if you were my girlfriend and then he said he has had you as his screensaver on his phone for the past year," Jay-O continued. "Uh? This sounds like a Lifetime movie," I said. "My first thought was to get a background check on the guy, but then I thought it's just a coincidence. There is no way he found out you lived here and then became my roommate to get closer to you," Jay-O said. Regardless if he did or not this guy who is apparently obsessed with me is now basically under the same roof as me especially since most of my belongings are at Jay-O's house now from staying almost every night. Jay-O ended up telling his aunt to do a background check on his roommate and there was nothing. My mind was calmer but when Jay-O's roommate was home I was not there unless Jay-O was there with me.

* * * * *

Once again I was feeling like I was not being the Christian I'm supposed to be and God was making me feel guilty for having sex before marriage. Jay-O turns me on. It's hard to say no, specially, when he rolls his eyes to the back of his head showing only the white part of his eyes. For some reason, that's so seductive to me predominantly because it showed me how engrossed he was at the moment. "Your body is so beautiful," he said. He loved my butt and my thighs, but unfortunately, I told Jay-O again we have to stop having premarital sex. He gets upset about it but eventually I would give in and we would have sex again, one day his roommate barged in on us. I think Jay-O was more embarrassed than I was. "He never knocks. If it's not Jesus watching us from the closet, it's my roommate walking in on us," Jay-O hissed.

* * * * *

We got into a habit of watching his favorite shows on TV while I massaged his feet. Most of his shows I would not watch if I were at my parents, but I have fun watching them with him. But it was something about watching movies with Jay-O. I would fall to sleep whenever we watched a movie. Jay-O expressed how displeased he was about it.

* * * * *

"Why don't you smile more," Jay-O asked. *I don't realize I'm not smiling until someone mentions it. Even if I'm thinking about flowers, I have a natural serious looking face*, I thought to myself, as we playfully chase and hit each other either at his place or the store. Danny disapproved of our playfully hitting each other, but we continued every chance we got, at least it made me smile more. We played my favorite game of Spades from time to time. This was when things were good. Jay-O had no reason to put me down or blame everything on me. But out of nowhere Jay-O would find a way to put me down. Call me a nigga or blame me for something. It's always my fault. *Man, I miss the good ole days when I was modeling, making money, and hanging out with the best of the best. How dare this boy treat me like this*, that was what was going on in my head anyways.

* * * * *

Ironically, as time went on Jay-O's roommate and I became close, though, I could tell he was growing feelings for me and his goal was to break Jay-O and me up. Little does he know Jay-O and I do that all on our own. But I could not fully trust his roommate especially since Jay-O had to stop him from googling me. I was flattered, to say the least, because Jay-O saw a guy interested in me and could be a possible threat. And now I had someone to confide in just like he had Vivian. She knows all of our business, specifically when we get into fights. He would come to tell me, "Vivian says I should apologize for the way I talked to you." The only time I get a break from her is when she goes to her other shop in Florida, then she's texting Jay-O. "You know she has you trained right," I said to Jay-O. "She told me how I should have you trained." He ignored me.

* * * * *

Jay-O's roommate and I became closer and closer, but it wasn't cute when Jay-O's roommate would plant something in Jay-O's head to start a fight between Jay-O and I. I warned Jay-O his roommate wants to break us up so he can be with me, but he replied, "My roommate does not want you." I left it alone.

* * * * *

Jay-O and I continued to constantly fight to the point where I thought I was beginning to age. He yelled at me on the phone and told me what a horrible person I am for working at the smaller hotel. "Well, at least I can buy my wine now. And why are you with me if I make you so unhappy," I asked. "Because we look good together," he answered. I told my aunt what he said, and for the first time, I could hear in her voice that she was disappointed in me because I won't leave him.

"Men like a strong woman, Monroe. You can't keep letting this guy run all over you," my friend said to me. I haven't talked to Brandon in ages. I gave him an update on my life. He was happy that I got a steady job, but my love life he was like, "Here we go again." Getting advice from my aunt or Penelope was cool but getting advice from a man's point of view other than my dad was better. I was hoping Brandon could help me break it off with Jay-O for good just like he helped me get away from Kelvin and all the other abusive men in my life. Yes, Jay-O is officially verbally and emotionally abusive to me and I don't like it one bit.

* * * * *

Jay-O's favorite manager is leaving the country for a few months which means Jay-O will be spending a lot more time at the store. One day I set up candles at the office to set a romantic scene while I helped him at the office until he found something I did wrong. "Don't forget to lock my office door!" he roared. There is a lot happening all at once at his store so yeah I forget once in a while but so does he. We argued all day. His new saying is, "I want to kill you." We laughed like we always do.

* * * * *

I hated when I left my stuff at his house because I never knew when we would break up and that was one thing he used to get us back together. It gave him time to apologize and to make it up to me. I'm so tired of his apologizes. His apologies remind me of my mom constantly apologizing to me. At least it confirmed that I was not overreacting and that they both are not very nice to me. I can't believe I finally was able to get away from my mom only to end up with a boyfriend just like her.

After a long day at the office he blurts, "All I want to do is go home, take a shower, and fuck." I rolled my eyes and argued, "I don't think it's cool for me to continue staying the night and having sex with you. There is no commitment between us. You could meet a younger girl next week and leave me. I don't have any security in this relationship. You want to act like we are married just without the ring!" He said to leave it alone because we have only been going out for six months. I agree, but I only bring up marriage when he wants sex. And not only that, we don't have to get married right away, but it would make me feel better if I knew my boyfriend wants to marry me one day. We dropped the conversation, when his brother text, resulting in him once again driving with one knee.

"My brother's girlfriend is a good one. Every time I go home we all hang out," Jay-O said when he hung up from his brother. "Happy to hear that," I said. On another note, Jay-O introduces me as his girlfriend now. Things were looking up for us but as soon as I think things are looking good and we are moving forward trouble arises. 'Watch what you speak out of your mouth Monroe. It could come true,' my mom always told me. The next day at Jay-O's office I was filing paperwork and I looked at his security camera and a young and beautiful Indian girl glides in his store like an angelic princess. I turned up the volume on his security system. She asked for an application and informed Jay-O his manager said she should stop in for work. She smiled and giggled the entire time and I could tell Jay-O was smitten and this was going to be trouble. There was one thing that appeased me and that she said she has a husband.

Chapter 12 - FEBRUARY

You have to give it to Jay-O. He doesn't joke with his after-work shower, and I find that very sexy that he keeps clean. He still smokes weed diligently. I don't talk about it with him. I know it's his getaway, considering the lingering issue with his staff stealing goods at the store and so on. Jay-O has really lost a fortune in the past month, and I wish I could help him somehow.

I have come to notice a bad habit, and now that I do, I wonder why it took me so long to see this. Right from the onset, Jay-O found a way to ruin big days for us. Public holidays, birthdays, and every other big day, except for Thanksgiving, we had a wonderful time. The customary fight before a big day happened again on the day that preceded the super bowl. We fought, and he left for DC. I stayed home with my dad to watch the super bowl. We got back together in his return from DC, as we always do after every fight.

* * * * *

Jay-O was contemplating hiring the young lady who came to the store last month. I wasn't too comfortable with that. I thought she was just too pretty for comfort. The only thing that abated my worry a little was my belief that she is married. However, our relationship isn't that solid to withstand storms like the temptation of a beautiful woman. Jay-O could get with the girl the next time we get in a fight. It turned out, the fight wasn't even far-fetched, as Jay-O had already hired the girl. We had another very heated argument, cussing at him asking God for forgiveness.

The new girl gave me plenty of sleepless nights. I plotted a scheme to get Jay-O's mind off of her. Not that the scheme will last too long, but it sure will buy me time. I knew the girl certainly would have eyes set on my man alright, but I told Jay-O his manager told the girl to come to the store to get an application just to prove to Jay-O that he knows pretty girls too. In fact, I made Jay-O believe his manager wanted to break us up so he could have me. I will have you know; that thing quickly went out of my hands. The girl was lovable and everyone liked her. Both customers and staff, and they all readily complimented her good looks. She even had an exotic name - Zara as they call her. Her smile is contagious, and even as a woman I love it. I found a customer who calls her smiley. This worried me, especially because Jay-O has always nagged about him wanting me to smile more.

In the coming weeks, Jay-O will brag about this new girl to his customers and staff. Singing her praises and telling me how cute she is. I will ask him why he's doing that, and he will say it's because she's smart and hard-working, unlike his other staffers who are full of drama. He had a point, she is hard-working, but that's not all the reasons he sings her praise. Jay-O is enamoured by this girl. I mean I see how he acts around her; like a teenager who's seeing a pretty girl for the first time. It disgusts me. I have been monitoring her very closely. She smiles at me, but I see something sinister behind that smile. A temptress with an eye of a tiger, just like the girl in Brazil. She's out for a rich guy to put all her burdens on. I am familiar with her kind.

* * * * *

Although Jay-O had been distracted by his 'smart' new employee, the thing with Vivian which I am not too clear on is still happening. Jay-O was to travel to Vegas, and surprisingly he called Vivian to drive him to the airport, and of course continue using his car while he's away. It infuriated me that he could choose another woman to bid him farewell on a trip. We broke-up again, right there and then. I darted out of the store and ignored his numerous calls. He left for Vegas, and for days we didn't communicate. When he finally texted me, it was to ask if I had taken care of the things he asked me to do, but I didn't as much as respond, until a couple of days before Valentine's Day. I broke down in tears when he said he will be heading to Chicago to pay his last respects to his grandfather who just passed. A grandfather I had never heard of, a grandfather whose burial Jay-O's younger brother wasn't going to attend. I was sure he was using this as an excuse to be away for Valentine's Day, but what could I do.

Meanwhile, at the hotel where I work, I met a charming guy named Lucas. I indulged myself and let him have my digits after several trials. I even spent a whole night chatting with him when I worked the overnight shift. I needed the distraction, especially with all that was going on with Jay-O. He offered to take me out on Valentine's Day and I agreed, but even though he's a cool person, I still had Jay-O on my mind. Jay-O and I spoke on Valentine's Day, and he almost killed himself when I told him I had plans for the night. I said that just to get him upset; I had already cancelled the date with Lucas. I enjoyed listening to him bluster over the phone. He somehow had to pay for hurting me all the time. He didn't even send me a flower for Val. He is so obsessed with that girl at the store. I'm sure of it.

We had another argument on his return from Vegas, mostly because he had no gifts for me, and he nagged about me not attending to the things he asked me to do while he was gone. I had enough of his bullshit, and so I ended it, and I told him it was for good. We could only stay away from each other for three weeks and for the first time instead of just calling and texting Jay-O came looking for me all apologetic and sorry. "I really miss you Monroe. I miss all of your ideas. The whole production babe." We got back together, and he confessed of making out in his office and in his car with the girl from his store. His argument, of course, was that it couldn't be called cheating since we were not together when it happened. I let it go, but couldn't understand why he wouldn't fire the girl, despite his excuse that she may accuse him of sexual assaulting her, claiming the girl is crazy.

Needless to say my aunt, mother, grandmother, and Brandon hates my relationship. "He is not going to marry you so why are you wasting your time," my grandmother said. They could always tell when we broke up. My whole demeanour would change. Every time we break up, I would tell them I'm not getting back with him, but then they find out we are back together. Now they don't believe what I say.

Chapter 13 - MARCH

Zara is officially a thorn in my flesh. Although she knows Jay-O and I are back together, she is after my man, and worst still, my man is letting himself fall for her. Jay-O never stopped referring to the kiss they shared and how her lips turned blue from the making-out, and how she thanked him for kissing her. I wish he will just stop. I found out she is not married, but she had a boyfriend of seven years who she broke up with just after a week of knowing Jay-O. I am determined to hold on tight to my man, but I wonder if it is worth it. Not only am I in contention with this new girl, but Vivian is also in the mix too. Jay-O wants it all. What a greedy bastard he is. I wish I didn't love him the way I do.

I met another man during our brief break up last month. His name is Jetty and he's the brother of my hot colleague at work. We vibed together quite easily, probably because he is into writing and the entertainment business like me. I'm enjoying the flirting, even though I know he's not enough to make me leave Jay-O.

* * * * *

Zara got back with her boyfriend eventually. The guy wanted to take his life because she left him. Jay-O implored me to make peace with her and I did, but she wouldn't stop calling and texting my man every night.

There's no way I can pretend to be friends with someone who's after my man. So, I resumed the malice. A call came in on Jay-O's phone some minutes past 10 pm one night. It was Zara. He said she was calling about her schedule. It just did not make any sense, and I felt so stupid and if Jay-O didn't think I was stupid, he wouldn't tell such a flimsy lie. We fought that night, and he punched a hole in the wall.

* * * * *

"I'm sorry baby, please don't leave. I know I was wrong and I admit it, even Vivian told me so," that was Jay-O apologizing to me the next day as I packed my things to leave for my grandmother's. How clueless can a man be to mention the name of another rival as an advocate for his woman? I let it go anyway, as Vivian wasn't my major problem. I asked him to stop communicating with Zara, and I hoped it will end there. It didn't. Days later, when I figured out the passcode to his phone, I went through his messages and saw several texts from her saying she loves him and offering him sexual favors. *How can I compete with a girl who is sluttier than the next slut*? I thought to myself. She stalked my social network page. It set me off. Of course, Jay-O shut me up when I asked about the texts and he changed his passcode too. I figured out the new passcode yet again, but his phone was clean. He had erased all correspondence between them.

I wanted Jay-O to fire Zara so bad, but he wouldn't. "She gives me evil looks, Jay-O," I said. His excuse was the same and he said, "She's a good worker, I may never find her type again. Will you work the cash register? No, right?" We quarrelled again when he made a silly remark about me having big dreams. "Zara works and she has big dreams to be a nurse. She is realistic. Are you?" It disgusted me to watch them work side by side. "I'm going to say something to this girl," I said. "You are wasting your time. She doesn't speak good English and besides I don't want her to file a lawsuit against me," he responded. It was hard to swallow what he said and even harder to erase the picture of them kissing from my head. I'm sure they still thought about it too.

Jay-O will say 'Thank you' every time I kiss him now, and it hurt. He picked the habit since he kissed Zara, and I begged him to stop haunting me with it, but he only said it more.

"You should leave him alone. He seems to have commitment issues and you are not his priority. He's so not good for you. I'm disappointed, though; I thought you guys were good for each other." Those were the words of my bestie when I gave her an update about my relationship with Jay-O. She was right, every time we get close he pulls away from me. He is emotionally unavailable and although he says he does not want to get married I think if he found the right girl he would marry her. He fails to believe I'm older than him and I know all of the games. But I can't figure out why I can't leave him. One thing's for sure, I will feel sorry for whoever his wife is going to be.

* * * * *

Jay-O came to see me at work after I began to work longer hours. He wanted to see the two other men I had mentioned to him. He met Lucas, whom he didn't see intimidated by. He feels more threatened by Jetty, but he hasn't gotten the chance to meet him yet. In turn, we begun a very weird sexual practice, where Jay-O fantasizes about Jetty having sex with me in the hotel while he is out of town. It was all so wrong, but it was fun too. The sex was so hot and amazing. Jay-O will leave work early so that we could have this fantasy sex, sometimes including Jetty's sister in the fantasy. We even did it over the phone when I had to leave town, and he climaxed three times. When it comes to this fantasy, I don't understand what drives us so crazy, and even though I have realized that we've fought less since we started it, something tells me God will end this soon.

Speaking of which, normally I have to say something about us having premarital sex, but before the end of the month, Jay-O stopped the fantasy, but why he did, I don't know. Jay-O just stopped. I guess he began to feel threatened by the fact that the thought of me and Jetty may come true.

I told Jetty I was back with Jay-O and we had to cancel a proposed trip just to avoid conflict with Jay-O, but he promised to keep flirting with me. I giggled.

Chapter 14 - APRIL

A few weeks after we stopped the sex fantasy thing, Jay-O attempted to re-ignite it, but I maintained that I'm not going down that road again. Nonetheless, we kept having sex now and then, but it was not as intriguing as the fantasy which lead us constantly arguing again. Now we do what we call JTT aka "Just the Tip," which means he does not put his sausage all in. But he would sneak and put his whole one-eyed German in me anyways making me not trust him. And it didn't help when I found out something rather disturbing, Jay-O has condoms hidden at every corner of his bed just for easy access. This seemed to me like he was all about my body.

Zara's continuous presence at the store is what we mostly argue about now. "Get over it already. Nothing is going on between Zara and me," Jay-O said. I could have been over the kiss by now but he has not given me the time to get over it because she is still around. Jay-O keeps saying how good she is for business and how she's improving his sales and profits in the short time she's been there. It drives me crazy. I understood his point, but he should have thought about his business before he had an intimate moment with her. I never see her text messages anymore, either he's deleting them, or they found other means to correspond and every time I remember that they kissed I lose control of my temper.

THE BREAKUP

* * * * *

As I said before, my boyfriend is a poor manager. I have watched closely how he runs his store, and I have mentioned it to him on a few occasions. He cussed me out and told me this is his business and not to tell him how to run it. It was obvious he didn't take me seriously, and I'm not surprised. He manages our relationship poorly, so, why wouldn't he run his store just the same. "You need to get back to that zoo you are running down there," Vivian said to Jay-O one day while he was at her store. He laughed and said you are right and I have to agree with that one too. But what triggered me the most is that he is evasive with me but takes other people's words with more value than mine.

* * * * *

I have come to find that Jay-O is more egoistic than I thought. He nurses his ego than anything else. I kid you not, let me tell you a story - a guy comes to play the guitar to entertain guests at my workplace. We got close. I could tell he liked me from the way he looked at me. Jay-O came in to see me at work one evening and the guitar guy got jealous, telling me he's a better man than my boyfriend. I told Jay-O what he said, and it turned out to be a mistake. Jay-O didn't like what he said at all, but I was shocked that he was mad at the guy because his ego was crushed, more than he was because another man liked me. You see what I mean?

* * * * *

Days passed and one morning Jay-O asked several unsettling questions about my plans for the day. It was unusual. We arrived at his store to meet auditors and of course Zara was there. One of the auditors' name was Cindy, and I pieced together the chat I saw on his computer back in September. Jay-O denied it but admitted it after much pressure. The girl had to leave for lunch but came back to complete the audit at the store, and I sliced around the corner and gasped as I caught a glimpse of them flirting, playing the same playful games we play when we are chasing and hitting each other. Jay-O flirts with almost every woman, and it is so annoying, remembering the time he flirted with a waitress at our favorite Mexican restaurant She was light skinned with big curly hair. She flirted back with him by playfully touching his hand and I threw my food at him. Anyway, back to this situation. I left the store in anger. When the auditing was over with, he said, "Relax, I just wanted to make sure she gave me a good report, so I did not owe any money after the audit like I did the last time. Remember I owed $8,000. It's business. That's all babe." He promised to cut communications with Cindy and that she wouldn't be coming to audit his store again.

Jay-O is full of lies, I can't trust him, especially with women. Furthermore, he isn't any better than the low lifers in the ghetto, even though he believes he's superior just because he has a few bucks. It's painful how on the outside things seem cool between us, and people walk in on us occasionally kissing and making out, but nobody has the faintest idea how bad he hurts me, and the things I put up with.

* * * * *

"I see you have abandoned us here. How very nice of you to check if we still exist." That was how my mom welcomed me when I visited them. I was guilty of not dropping by, but I talk to her on the phone all the time. I avoid seeing her as much as I can, just because of her drama. "How's that boyfriend of yours? You know he hasn't come here to visit. I'm not sure if you're hiding him from us, or he doesn't recognize us. You shouldn't be staying in his house you know? It's not right." Mother wouldn't stop. It was hard to stop her once she started speaking her mind. There was some truth in what she said, though, but I've grown fond of Jay-O, I can't just stay away from him. He needs me around. I have to look after him, as he can hardly do anything for himself. I actually rock him to sleep some nights, just like a baby. This made me further believe Jay-O is spoiled and even though his mom is not around he seems like a mama's boy.

Speaking of family, Jay-O's family are going to be in town for a few days, and his brother is going to introduce his girlfriend of three months to them. I found this out by eavesdropping on a phone conversation between him and his brother. Jay-O had asked if I was interested in attending an event with him, his brother, and his girlfriend, but he said nothing about his family. I asked him why he kept this a secret, and why he wouldn't introduce me to his family when his brother was ready to do so with his girlfriend of three months and we have been dating way longer than that. "I told you how my family feels about the kind of girl they want me with. My brother doesn't care what they say and my brother wants to get married. I'm not my brother," he answered. Jay-O and I got confrontational, but eventually he agreed to introduce me to them. I did not get the expected excitement since he didn't do it willingly.

* * * * *

History happened. Our city had its first riot due to police brutality. Jay-O's store was hit amongst a few others in the neighborhood. Vivian's store was untouched. His aunt believes his store was targeted because he treats some of his undesirable customers like crap like he does his employees. "The Black people steal from me just like my Black employees," he said. I understand, but there is a proper way to handle things. I was there to clean up the mess, but Vivian and Mallory got the praise for just picking up the mop for two-minutes and comforting him but I was the one getting my hands dirty.

* * * * *

Jay-O wants me to stop drinking. We've been going back and forth on the issue for months. He believes wine makes me mouthy, but he's wrong. I speak my mind whether or not I am under the influence, but the wine does help me express what's been on my mind for a long time.

* * * * *

He's grown so much since we met though. He has added more weight and has a lot of facial hair too. Sadly, Jay-O's brain and mind still work like a toddler's. *We don't need to have a child. I already have one*. I thought to myself.

* * * * *

He got on my nerves again when he said none of my ideas has turned into money yet and that I have to get a new job. "I dumped the other girls I was dating when I met you because I thought you had it going on and was buying a house," Jay-O said. *I remember telling him at one point in my life I was about to move in his neighborhood, but things obviously did not work out. But that was a long time ago and that is what he was basing our relationship on*, I thought to myself. "I need you to get another job. I'm sick of paying for all of the dinners and you are ungrateful," he continued. "Ungrateful! I'm very grateful. I appreciate everything you do for me!" I exclaimed.

He insisted I was ungrateful, but seriously I don't need all of these dinners and besides I thought that is what men do. He acts like I'm asking him for a Louis Vuitton bag. Guys have been paying for dinners for me for years hoping that one day I would be their girl. This dude has me and he doesn't know how to treat me.

Jay-O has never brought me anything nice beside the time Vivian invited us to her trunk show. But his end game was to get me close to Vivian so she can come around when she feels like it and use his vehicle without me saying anything. Not only that her agenda is to get me comfortable enough to open up to her, so she gets all of my business and then use it against me to get my man. She is so textbook on how to break a couple up and he is constantly trying to convince me that she wants to be friends with me so I said to Jay-O. "No, she doesn't want to be friends with me, she wants to be your friend. I know I can be sceptical, but I know girls like her," and then he had the nerve to say Vivian told him, "I don't want to get too close to Monroe unless you are going to marry her." Exactly what I thought she wants to be close enough to learn my business but not close enough to be a real friend unless I get married to Jay-O? I don't want her phony friendship.

* * * * *

I wish Jay-O would love me for me and leave me alone about getting another job. "You need to put

80% of your time into a steady job and 20% into your hobby," he said. He had a point there and I know I'm getting older, so I need to use my college degree or put more effort into the entertainment business, but I will do it in my time not in Jay-O's time. To appease the situation I gave him a deadline on when I would get a better job.

On the other hand, I don't see him complaining when his friend from DC comes to visit him on Tuesday nights. "Turn it up Tuesdays!" he announced. He waits for me to get off of work at 11:30 pm so I can pick his drunk ass up from the casino. One night he was so drunk he got down on one knee and proposed to me. I could not settle him down until 4:30 am and I had to be back at work at 7:30 am. He was loud and embarrassing. Running out into the street butt naked.

Picking him up from the casino happened a few times. One night Vivian was in the mix. She, Jay-O, and his friend from DC went out for crabs to talk about the riot. He claims he eventually sat at the bar drinking while she ate crabs on her own. "Before we became a couple, did you two go out before," I asked and he said no. Just what I thought. But what disturb me the most was that she did his hair by putting it up in a ponytail that evening. I told him if she ever touched him again it was over for good. He agreed but I'm beginning to see what this relationship really is - a parasite. It drains me of all my energy, and how can I be productive when all I spend time doing is fighting and arguing with my man. A man who never supports me in anything I do. All he does is find faults and talk down to me.

On top of that, even though I'm Jay-O's girlfriend he continues to think he is God's gift to women and he has admitted he uses his charm to get what he wants. Like I said before, he seems to be getting more and more attention. Ever since he has been with me, he is sociable and likable at the store and in the neighborhood. He enjoys it and in turn, he shows off at work. "Well, at least you know where he is," my aunt said to me. Little does she know his store is his playground. The girls love him especially the Black girls. They know a cash cow when they see one and the good hair is the icing on the cake.

* * * * *

Most of the time I ignore Jay-O but he knows just what to say to get me started, more of the reason how he reminds me of my mom. But again he knows how to be nice and turn my tears into smiles as we took snap shots in a photo booth. We had a strip of cute and funny faces. I posted up on his refrigerator.

* * * * *

I found myself confiding in Jay-O's roommate more and more. He is a cool person. Easy to chat with but there was one thing me and Jay-O did not like and that he had an uncomfortable stare. Regardless, we were becoming closer. Jay-O's roommate knows about Zara and he wondered why I stayed. "Men like to hump," he said, and we laughed simultaneously. But I know it's up to me to let Jay-O go and I know he is a jerk but he is my jerk. Speaking of being a jerk, Jay-O continues to go home on the weekends without me; *I'm breaking up with him when he gets back*, I thought to myself. As soon as he comes back, he is hung over from drinking and taking hard drugs. "Can you take care of me?" he asked. And I would fall for it every time.

He is still constantly asking what am I getting for his birthday and reminding me I missed his birthday last year. He irritates me when he says I did not get him anything.

* * * * *

Now the employees including my manager know about us and word travelled like a rollercoaster. "Ask your boyfriend can I get a discount on an iPad," one of my employees said. Jay-O is not that type of person. When he visited me at work the guys know who he is but they still would try to get my number. They saw him as no threat. And of course, the question I have been dreading, "Why do work here if your boyfriend owns a store?"

At first, my employees thought I was in a happy relationship, but my manager could tell something was wrong based on my job performance. I began to confide in her and another employee that works with me who is going through the same drama with her man. I knew it was not the wisest thing to do but I knew my family and friends was tired of hearing about my relationship problems with Jay-O, including my cousin who now worked at the hotel with me. But before he worked at the hotel, I got him a job with Jay-O. After two weeks my cousin was out of there. "He may be getting over on the foreigners that work for him but he ain't getting over on me. He better pay me my money or else," my cousin said. "And you need to leave that punk alone."

* * * * *

Jay-O continues to remind me not to lock the keys in his office especially since his manager is now officially gone which means Zara will be working with him more often with just them two at times. "Lord I ask for your mercy and forgiving me for being in a relationship like this. I know you are not pleased and I have no idea why I stay. Please help."

* * * * *

"Can I use your computer?" Jay-O asked. I hated it when he used my stuff because he didn't take care of it, so we fought about it. I don't care; we can fuss all night because I know he will not replace it even though he owns an electronic store.

* * * * *

Despite our arguments and breaking up Jay-O has a sense of humor. He would make me laugh so hard my eyes would tear up. His roommate would have to come and see what is so funny at times. I remember one day a cop came in Jay-O's store to follow up on a shoplifting issue. "Yeah, a guy stole some stuff from me. He was also lurking near my girlfriend's job," Jay-O said. He made the shoplifter look like the scariest shoplifter out there, so the cop asked, "Do you want to make a report?" Jay-O said yes. "What did he steal?" the officer wondered. "He stole a bag of chips and a snickers bar from the front counter," Jay-O responded. The officer and I laughed and laughed. I thought he stole a smartphone and some more stuff. From the look on Jay-O's face, he was not happy and did not find it funny, so the officer wrote up the report and went on his way. During this time, Jay-O reminded me of Michael from one of his favorite shows, *The Office*.

* * * * *

Jay-O was upset after finding a text message from Jetty. "Oh, you were going on a trip with him?" Jay-O said. See the thing about Jay-O is that he can do whatever he wants to me, but he can't handle me doing anything to him. "I cancelled that trip," I said. He argued with me all night. I reminded him that he still works with the girl he kissed. The next day he left me on the doorstep of my family's home while he went to DC to see his brother and his girlfriend. I waited in the cold until my parents returned.

* * * * *

The door to Jay-O's office slammed behind me and the unthinkable happened. I paused while my heart beat as fast as a roadrunner. I ran to the front of the store to find Jay-O, but I saw someone comforting for the moment. "Danny you won't believe what just happened. I locked the keys in the office," I said. Danny shook his head, he knew what was coming next as Jay-O stood behind me. "Tell him," Danny said. As soon as I told Jay-O where his keys were, he flipped out, cussing and calling me all sorts of names. I ran out the store to see if I could find a locksmith. I stumbled upon one store, but the locksmith was busy. I begged and begged until he made time to come to Jay-O's store. I paid $150 from my pocket. When we arrived, Jay-O was sitting in his office as if nothing happened. "Oh, I had an extra key in my safe. Where did you go?" Jay-O asked. *That bastard*, I thought to myself. "What kind of boyfriend do you have?" the locksmith said on his way out the door.

Chapter 16 - MAY

There were so many formalities about meeting Jay-O's family. The list of dos and don'ts was long enough to fill a brochure. I was certain I wouldn't even remember half of it. Jay-O pointed out what I could and couldn't wear mainly because his great aunt is very hard to please. Meeting his brother was all I relished, and it turned out to be somewhat a disappointment. He wasn't as happy to meet me. Obviously, Jay-O had told him negative things about me. But thanks to his girlfriend Misty, she told him to give me a chance and to make me feel welcome. That was nice of her but Jay-O can still be an idiot when he really wants to be, but I couldn't have imagine he could pick such a moment as my meeting with his family to be an ass.

It was a Wednesday, and we waited in the store for them to join us before taking the gathering elsewhere. They wanted to see the store and see how well their nephew was doing. Jay-O managed to fray my nerves by fighting with me right before we received his aunt and uncle at the door. The fury was good for me in the end. It killed my anxiety, and even though I had to feign a smile to welcome them, everything went smoothly between us. It was quite a relief. I was totally ignorant of the fact that there were more coming. More aunts, cousins, uncles and relatives, including his mom and dad. More than I could imagine. More than my boyfriend prepared me for. I was surprised when I got to his apartment later to meet what seemed like a crowd of Asians.

I managed to keep my composure anyway. Jay-O made a silly joke about me probably wanting to appear taller than I am before everyone, and so I could keep my heels on instead of taking them off at the entrance as is the usual practice. I took them off anyway before his Aunt Taka asked me too. I was glad I had done so already.

Misty and I cooked. I liked her immediately. She seemed like a simple person and eventually I wanted to thank her for talking to Jay-O's brother about me, as Jay-O stood in the kitchen snacking on what was already cooked. His Aunt Taka didn't seem to like Jay-O's roommate as she gave him a nasty look and said, "我不喜欢他的凝视." What did she just say Jay-O," I whispered. "She does not like my roommates stare," Jay-O replied. I get it, but we were used to that already. We all ate at Jay-O's condo. Aunt Taka didn't even offer Jay-O's roommate any food, which to me was a bit rude, but of course, I said nothing.

I heard Jay-O's great aunt later in the evening saying she wouldn't sleep in Jay-O's room because we were having pre-marital sex. I wish I could explain to her that it was her great-nephew who has been pushing me to have sex with him all the while. Not that it could change anything, I just wanted my name cleared. His parents seemed to like me. They did not seem as big and bad as Jay-O made them but there was so much scrutiny. It was as though Jay-O was a little child that couldn't be trusted with his life.

Jay-O had long taken off our pictures from the fridge, because he thought they were disrespectful due to us kissing in one of them. Aunt Taka came into the room that evening and I was sure she was snooping around. She did find my things that I had hidden away in Jay-O's closet, and she didn't look pleased, as Misty said, "Let's go to the mall."

I tagged along with Misty, Jay-O and his brother to the mall to get her a dress for the event we were all going to the next day. But I tagged along so that I could get a chance to get along with his brother. This was important to me because Jay-O looked up to his younger brother. Odd. But anyway, Jay-O and Misty had plenty of time to bond over the months on his several trips to DC. Misty and Jay-O also texted throughout the week. I was the outcast, and I wanted to change that status fast.

"What do you think about all this?" Misty whispered to me after dragging me aside just before we hit the road to the mall. I wasn't sure what she meant, so I asked: "About what?" "About this family" she added, I was clueless about what she meant. "I don't know; I just met them," I said, and got into the car. It was a weird scene, and I'm not sure what to make of it. The ride to the mall was fun. Jay-O calling me out my name jokily wasn't fun. This was the first time he would do that in front of others.

I told a joke about how Jay-O's chips were stolen by a neighborhood thug. We all had a good laugh. I personally almost couldn't catch my breath. Once again, Jay-O did not find it funny.

Upon arrival at the mall. Jay-O and I shopped, and got goodies for Jay-O's brother and his girl. They loved it. I soon sensed though, that they seemed to have had an argument, from the way Misty walked superfast ahead of her boyfriend, and Jay-O's next action did not help the situation.

Man, the things Jay-O does sometimes are so unbelievable. He is insensitive, this I know. His brother gave me his sweater when I got cold on our way from the mall, and I told Jay-O later that his brother is cute. Jay-O couldn't pick a better time to tell his brother than when his girl was right there. I wish I weren't there to see the look in her eyes when she heard what I said about her boyfriend.

His brother seemed to be cool with me so far, but now I had my sights set on Misty. Something told me she was up to some mischief. We stopped to shop for ingredients for our lunch for the event. Jay-O and his brother wanted to buy things they needed to make a pizza. I was excited about that since that is my favorite food. It's a tradition for them, to make a huge pizza with all sorts of goodies on it and I was told not to get involved in the making of it. *No problem, I just like to eat it,* I thought to myself.

Before heading back home after shopping, Misty and Jay-O stopped to get a sandwich at a shop she heard about, and I got a chance to be alone with his brother. We nattered a bit and mostly waited in silence.

Misty will later brag about a huge party they had planned for Jay-O's birthday, and how much fun it was going to be. She kept on about it, without mentioning or inviting me, like I was not there, and worse still, Jay-O said nothing to change the tune. I can't find words to express my embarrassment. What kind of man doesn't stick up for his woman in a situation like that? I will tell you. Jay-O is that kind of person.

We returned to Jay-O's condo and his place was empty. His family went back to DC but his aunt and uncle are coming back in a few days which left us alone to cook and to get to know each other more. By this time Misty had other things on her mind. "I want to do something special for your brother's birthday and I may need your help," I said to Jay-O's brother while Jay-O was in the bathroom. "Oh, yeah, what?" Misty answered instead. After explaining the gift, she realized it had to do with Jay-O's favorite things and she tested me by saying, "So, what are his favorite things?" I politely changed the subject. I had no need to prove anything to her. I sat on the couch thinking

Misty would join me so the brothers could cook but instead she helped out making me look like a lazy bum and Jay-O said nothing. "I thought this was something you guys did together?" I said. Misty stopped helping and stood in the kitchen staring at them making the pizza. *This girl I thought was simple is a bitch*, I thought to myself.

Misty facetimed her family once again leaving me out. Jay-O did finally introduce me. "Oh she is beautiful," Misty mom said to Jay-O. Misty in fury. "Thank you," I smiled, but then I felt sick realizing that everyone had a tight relationship that I wanted so badly, but Jay-O was not letting it happen. He was not taking up for me or making me feel welcomed. It was all about Misty and his brother.

I went to lie down and from the kitchen, I could hear Misty gossiping about Jay-O's family. "Your aunt is so mean. I could not believe she did not offer your roommate any food," Misty said. I just knew Jay-O was about to lit into her like he does me when I talk about his family, especially his aunt, but nothing. He agreed with Misty. Now I was furious.

A couple of hours later Jay-O and I left. We stayed at my hotel to give Misty and his brother space. The next morning I told Jay-O to go to the event without me because I was not feeling well. He was upset and said I have to go because of the amount of money he spent on the tickets. He left me no choice but to tell him I did not like Misty which made him even more upset. "I let my guard down thinking your brother's girlfriend was a nice person from what you have been telling me for all of these months. She is just the opposite, and I don't think it's a good idea for me to spend the whole day with her," I confessed. "You are going, now get dressed," he demanded, and just like that we left.

Our PDA was heavy in the car on the way to the event but all of a sudden Jay-O stops and shouts, "Oh shit I forgot our tickets, turn the car around!" We ended up at my job so I could run upstairs to retrieve the tickets. In a matter of minutes, I'm standing in front of my job and the car is gone. My phone rings and I see Jay-O's name across my caller ID. "Hello?" I said. "Meet me in front of my store," he replied. I rushed to his store and Jay-O is nowhere to be found. "He is at The Playhouse," several of the neighbors shout from across the street. Jay-O comes dashing out and said, "Vivian let me print the tickets." I wanted to sit on the curb and give up on Jay-O but as usual, I said nothing and we drove off.

Jay-O would later tell me his brother said he could not believe he calls me bitches, sluts, and nigga. He explained that's how we joke around but deep down inside I knew it was wrong.

"Doesn't she act like Aunt Taka," Jay-O said to his brother after we had an argument about getting him more beer while sitting at the event picnic style. He ignored him and suggested they walk the event grounds. Misty and I waited for their return. She asked about my career. We talked and I thought maybe now we could get to know each other but she stared and cut her eyes at me and I knew this girl was no good and Jay-O's brother better watch out.

Jay-O and his brother returned and if I was not mistaken Misty was flirting with Jay-O, but it all came to a halt when she grabbed my man's hand after he had a drunken episode with another event attendee. I know when to stop my man. Believe me; I have been around enough of his drunken episodes during casino night. Needless to say, I cussed Misty out.

By the night end, Jay-O left me in the hotel bawling while they all went out to dinner. I looked so bad in front of Jay-O's brother. His brother wondered what happened to me and Jay-O blamed everything on me. His brother never wanted to see me again and come to find out Misty was intimated by me because Jay-O's brother cheated on her early in their relationship and she was scared he may have liked me after I had said he was cute. She saw me as a threat but the deed was done and now I wanted nothing to do with her. Misty is a born snake. Besides, I found out later she had already been to China to meet Jay-O's parents. *They had a special dinner together and all. I met his family at the store and later had a casual gathering at his place with his roommate and his stare? That wasn't anything special*; I thought to myself. She had no reason to be intimated by me. Furthermore, Jay-O's brother was obviously into her unlike Jay-O is with me.

The next day, Jay-O's brother and Misty went back to DC and his aunt returned with family members but not the ones I had already met. I chatted with his aunt some and she mentioned that Misty is a bitch and she wished Misty did not leave London to move in with her nephew. I was so glad to know I was not overreacting.

His Aunt Taka asked me for a favor. She explained to me that Jay-O needed help at the store, so that is why she brought his other aunt, uncle, and their son. She needed to see if they could stay at my hotel. My manager agreed to let them stay for free for thirty days. They were happy but in a few days the store ended up being robbed twice, go figure; and according to their son he said to Jay-O and I, "My dad thinks there are too many Black people around. Just too many Black people." He kept saying it until Jay-O finally said to him, "You know my girlfriend is Black." He turned red as a beet and said, "I didn't know she is Black. She doesn't look Black." We laughed hysterically. Needless to say, they returned to DC.

I don't think Jay-O is cut out for the store," his mom was telling his aunt. She agreed but had no choice but to let Jay-O continue to run it whether or not his family stayed.

Since his brother did not help me regarding Jay-O's birthday present, I asked his Aunt Taka. She was no help either and all she was worried about was getting a man that is about to turn 30-years-old a new car. *I can see doing something like that for a teenager or someone in their twenties but for a grown man who has the money to do it. No wonder Jay-O is egotistic and spoiled*, I thought to myself. But I was shocked when she told me everything is in her name. The store, his condo. Jay-O doesn't own anything. *Mr. I'm worth $600,000 and you have nothing speech all day almost every day,* I thought to myself. His family could drop him tomorrow and he would be left with nothing and he has the nerve to talk about me. Now I'm beginning to think he does not want me to get a job to better my life but he needs me to get a job to take care of him.

* * * * *

"Someone always quits when my aunt is here for a visit. She is always so hard on my employees. I can't stand her sometimes. She's crazy," Jay-O raved. That only meant Zara would be working, even more, hours. She is a fixture at his store. His aunt does not care for her though. She thinks just the opposite of what Jay-O thinks about Zara and that she is a poor worker and stupid. But it does not matter Jay-O and I continue to fight over Zara. One day Zara and I bumped into each other like a stagnant rubber car in a suffocating hallway. She gave me a hateful look.

There was one thing that made my day. Zara is now engaged and she is leaving next month to go to Indian for three months to marry her fiancé. "Are you happy now, Monroe?" Jay-O said. It annoyed me that she left on her accord instead of Jay-O firing her months ago. His excuse was still that he needed her services at the store. "And what's going to happen when she returns in three months? Are you going to hire her back?" I asked. He boasts he's not going to rehire her on her return, but Jay-O has no honor, I can't take his word for it. Jay-O and I fault so bad over these questions we broke up and this time I would not get back with him so he played his ace card and said he would marry me. We got back together, but the marriage proposal was short-lived.

It was yet another holiday and instead of Jay-O starting an argument Vivian invited us to her Memorial Day cookout. We did not go but I know he wanted too.

Chapter 17 – JUNE

We continued to do the JTT but ended up having sex, and Jay-O actually blames me for it. "You wait so long to do the JTT so yeah I put my dick in you," Jay-O said. It doesn't get to me though, as it is the least of his wrong doings. My self-esteem has once again taken a serious dent from his fault finding in everything I do, and his insulting remarks. Sometimes it hits me too hard and I leave him, and in a few days, I'm back in his arms. I must say though; he still does not give me the chance to follow through with my decision to end the relationship. He begs like a child that needs money for candy. He continues to seize my belongings sometimes, including my driver's license or credit cards just to make sure I have reason to see him, and when I do, like I said, he falls at my knee and begs. *I need to listen to my advice in my play*, I thought to myself.

From the look of things, it's safe to say his family likes me, although his father thinks we are friends, I could sense a bit of resentment on a couple of occasions. They had reservations about how I lived with him and was doing less with my life and that I need a better job. *It's funny how they are putting down the job that was going to let their family stay for free?* I thought to myself. But anyway, I'm working on seriously getting a better job now. I need to get something going on for myself. Jay-O says he needs a partner, and now he says if I get a job that guarantees my financial stability, he'll walk down the aisle with me. My thoughts are different. I think it shouldn't matter that much to him if he truly loved me.

Jay-O still wouldn't let me speak my mind when it comes to his family. He shuts me up before I open my mouth. I had to mock him once though, about how Misty spoke openly about her thoughts of the family and he didn't stop her. Of course, it stung him and we had another fight. But he did agree that Misty is a bitch, but he has to like her because it's important to his brother. I then said, "Well your brother is not worried about liking me?" Jay-O was silent.

To make my life better, I began to move my stuff out of Jay-O's house a little at a time. I think his family's reaction towards my living with him when I'm not his wife was all the awakening I needed. I have them to thank for that, but I did put our picture back on the fridge. I'm not allowing any girl come in there thinking my man is single.

On the bright side, after several cancelled trips and delays, Zara left for Indian and it made me wonder now if his business would fail during her absence since he needs her services so badly. Of course, there is more to his desire to keep her around than meets the eye. Anyway, three months without the girl around is quite refreshing, so I take solace in that. It left me with just Vivian to deal with, which turned out to be a handful. She overheard my boyfriend and I discussing my displeasure about him letting her use his car all the time. Jay-O talked down about her, called her a bitch, and said he wouldn't allow her to use his car again, but then snuck over to her store to settle with her, leaving me out as the bad guy.

To make manners worst he kept giving her the car without my knowledge, through a text message I found. He would let her know when I was at the store and when I wasn't so she would know when to come to get the car. It is bad already that he can't stand his ground and follow through with what we agreed on, Jay-O made it worse by keeping the goings on between them a secret. I couldn't overlook that, and we fought seriously over it. He shouted at me like a teenager that needed some scolding, telling me about how his car and everything he owns belongs to him and not me. In turn, he can do what he wants I felt unwanted, bashed, and disrespected. Relationships aren't meant to be this way. I broke-up with him yet again.

Jay-O kept calling, and at a point he threatened to kill me if I wouldn't let him see me. I found it funny. It only showed his level of frustration, how much he'd missed me, and how useless he is without me. Instead of answering his phone calls, I went to his store eventually, and we settled again.

* * * * *

Jay-O out of his lack of sensitivity told me about how Zara had been calling him from Indian. I did not make a huge fuss out of it. According to him, she wanted Jay-O to leave me for her, if not she is going through with her wedding. *She is such a little girl*, I thought to myself, as a secured call came in while we was sitting in his office. Jay-O took the call, and it was from her, but that was no big deal. What irked me was that he got up and left the office to take her call. I waited for him to return, and ranted like a mad dog before storming out of his store. He came to me, explaining that he told her to get married and forget about him, but I didn't believe that. He wouldn't have had to step out if that was what he was going to say to her. In fact, I believe he would have preferred to say it in my presence just to prove a point. I left without looking back and got a text from him moments later. 'I will send your nude pictures to your parents if you don't come back' the text read. I got a huge kick out of it. It was a lame bluff; he had no nude pictures of me.

On the other hand, love makes us foolish sometimes. We got back together, and I spent the night at his condo again, to wake up the next morning to find Jay-O taking pictures of me in bed. I was totally unclad. I felt stupid, but isn't that what love is meant to be? "I'm a model remember? Make me famous like one of those reality stars, I'll be very grateful," was all I said.

"Oh now you are grateful," he said, as he deleted the pictures right away, but I'm not sure why. It's hard to tell; maybe he felt threatened by the prospect of me being famous like a reality star.

* * * * *

I was sad to see Jay-O's roommate leaving. He was fed up with Jay-O bullshit too and our constant fights. Surprisingly, Jay-O did admit keeping the girl at the store was wrong and he apologized. "You better not rehire her when she returns if you do I will have her deported," I threatened and he laughed. Now Jay-O has a new excuse for not marrying me. He says his brother is probably going to marry Misty and since Misty is a white girl it's up to him to marry an Asian girl to please his parents. "I thought you did not want to get married or if I get a better job then we can get married. Which one is it?" I said. He recanted and said you know what I mean. I said, "I believe I don't."

* * * * *

One day Danny pulled me to the side and said, "Now that Jay-O's family likes you, to stay in good with his family you need to get a better job." *Honestly, I don't know how much longer I can deal with Jay-O. If he would stop running after me when we break up I would have been gone,* I thought to myself. "I'm not worried about his family and if Jay-O doesn't get it together I'm leaving for LA at the end of this month," I said to Danny in frustration. "I hear you. Jay-O smokes, drinks, and takes drugs, so what are you going to do with that anyways? Make up your mind on what you need to do because as far as I'm concerned, Jay-O should have been enrolled in the army to teach him how to be a man," Danny said. That was funny coming from a man who told Jay-O I was not the right girl for him.

* * * * *

Ever since his family left, he is on me about the way I dress. His mother stated I dress too much like a model. I knew she was going to say that when I saw his mother staring me down in my fitted jeans.

* * * * *

My job definitely knows that Jay-O is abusive especially since he hangs up in my manager's ear when he's looking for me after we break up. My co-worker saw him hanging around our parking lot through the security camera. My manager said he does not love me and he will never marry me. She says she knows because she use to be a Jay-O. She was blunt like that. I continued to get advice from her. I never told them about Zara. I was too embarrassed.

Now my manager does not like him mainly because he would not give her a charger for her phone and now she takes it out on me? She doesn't understand that Jay-O is not giving like that and when his aunt was here I see where he gets it from.

* * * * *

Can I think of one reason to stay with Jay-O, I thought to myself. I can never come up with one. Jay-O has adopted a new saying that he jokily says and that is he hates me.

* * * * *

"My mom is getting me a new car for my birthday. I am not putting you on my insurance. I'm not letting anyone drive my new car not even Vivian," Jay-O said. So basically, I can drive his raggedy car just not the new one? Once upon a time, I would not be caught dead in a beat up car such as his, but I sucked it up just to be with him. I ignored him.

* * * * *

Jay-O is still smoking, taking his faithful showers, asking me what I am going to do for his 30th birthday, and bringing up my job situation and how much he spent on dinners a year ago. I'm still falling asleep during movies and drinking my wine. Shamefully, we still argue about Vivian and Zara even though she is gone. According to the outsiders looking in Jay-O is a spoiled, immature, narcissistic manipulator, who hides behind the boy next door look, and that I need to get out of this toxic relationship. But I can't. I'm pregnant.

To be continued…

THE BREAKUP

Brooke Gantt

is an author & modelpreneur who has been featured in some of the hottest magazines in the world, graced the runways of some of the most exclusive fashion shows, and appeared in numerous commercials and television shows. She has written several fan favorite novels, short stories, and more! She lives in New York City.

"THE GOOD, THE BAD, THE UGLY…"

Elizabeth Tight has a secret life that is not so glamorous. This erotic and suspenseful novel is filled with celebrity and reckless relationships. From teenage abuse to adulthood drama, dirty little secrets, lies, and juicy sex scandals, *Secret Chronicles of a Fashion Model: The Fugitive's Girlfriend* is guaranteed to keep your eyes glued to the pages.

This twisted tale is also a conversational story of romance and danger. Is it truth or fantasy? You decide. Let the crime mystery begin!

Shhhh, don't tell…

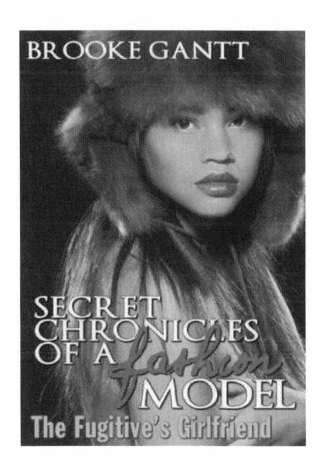

Read on for a special excerpt from the fascinating
Elizabeth Tight story, available at

www.ModelShrink.com

Secret Chronicles of a Fashion Model: The Fugitive's Girlfriend

Introduction

"Stop! Please, stop! I won't do it again!" Elizabeth cried. She screamed in pain with terror in her eyes. The rage in Elizabeth's voice was not being used to fight for world peace but to persuade her boyfriend Casmir from choking her with a cord and sexually attacking her.

"Shut up!" he growled. A flood of tears gushed down her red flushed cheeks. Elizabeth screamed louder, as the phone cord wrapped tighter around her neck. Her boyfriend's one-eyed snake protruded deeper into her bruised anal cavity, face down, ass up. She dares not move, in fear of being slapped in the back of her head by his unforgiving hand.

Thus far, this was the most degrading abuse Elizabeth had endured by Casmir. The gun he once pointed at her or the pillow he suffocated her with until he decided Elizabeth could breathe again could not even compare. The feeling...the reckless pain at its best would be hard to describe, but Casmir knew having sex through the back door was the worst kind of intercourse for her, so he used it for punishment.

Even so, it still did not stop Elizabeth from rashly returning to Casmir's arms, shamefully happy they were still together.

"I love you," Casmir whispered by her ear.

"I – love – you, too," Elizabeth murmured slowly.

"Don't ever go to the store again without asking me, first," he said. Elizabeth and Casmir made love like nothing ever happened.

As the plot thickens, this shocking, unforgettable, and emotional rollercoaster ride of love will reveal a chain of events that no one should ever have to endure. Leave your comfort zone and get ready to enter the unbelievable and unreal wilderness of a manhunt with blood at the end, involving a lost but beautiful, biracial 15-year-old young lady. She goes by the name Elizabeth Tight... not Liz or Beth, just Elizabeth.

DID MONROE AND JAY-O FINALLY BREAK UP OR DID SOMETHING MORE SINISTER HAPPEN?

Stay Tuned!

Read this jaw-dropping drama filled novel *The Breakup Part Two* coming soon at

www.ModelShrink.com

EVER MISSED OUT ON AN OPPORTUNITY AND WISHED YOU COULD GET IT BACK?

Honey did. She missed out on the biggest opportunity of her life the day NBA player Shaq walked into her life. Will supermodel Honey get that life changing experience again? Read this fun, adventurous, and comedic romance now and find out!

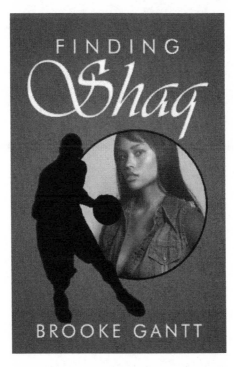

Check out this fun, adventurous, and comedic romance now and find out available at

www.ModelShrink.com

MEN...SMH

These unforgettable short stories and monologues are based on men and events women can relate too.

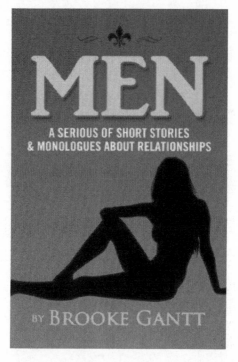

Leave your comfort zone and get ready to enter shocking stories that are told through the eyes of a colorful character named Chocolate, available at

www.ModelShrink.com

OTHER TITLES:

How to Become a Model in 28 Days

How to Become a Christian Model in 28 Days

Fashion Model Survival Guide: How to Avoid

Pitfalls & Scams

Model Shrink: Top 10 Tips & Tricks to Losing Weight

Without Working Out

Children's Book – Brooke & Ki

Visit www.ModelShrink.com for more details.

Proof

Made in the USA
Charleston, SC
27 February 2017